Socrates

Uncle Gnarls

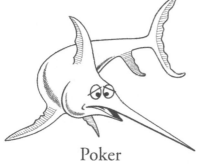

Poker

Bondar

Amaya

Noni

Serine

Little Peetie

Zippee

Kaihula

Jacko

Shredder

Two Stars

Tooney and Schooner

Dimension of Terror

Book Three: The Adventure Continues

Thomas McGee

authorHOUSE®

AuthorHouse™
1663 Liberty Drive
Bloomington, IN 47403
www.authorhouse.com
Phone: 1-800-839-8640

Published by AuthorHouse   10/09/2012

ISBN: 978-1-4772-7218-3 (sc)
ISBN: 978-1-4772-7217-6 (hc)
ISBN: 978-1-4772-7216-9 (e)

Library of Congress Control Number: 2012917468

A Note from the Author

The uncertainty and daily tragedies of our time should peak our awareness to the world around us. Whether young or old, our lives cannot focus only on ourselves and the pursuit of vain entitlements as the negative influence spawned by such a mindset destroys the fabric of any society. Regardless of our station in life, nothing can replace hard work. It is a necessary and strategic component in the foundation for anyone's personal self-esteem and subsequent success.

The Socrates adventure series is an effort to turn complacency into positive action, encouraging the reader to think about our beautiful planet as a shared experience. Our personal actions and reactions should always include the benefit to

others. The simple Hawaiian phrase for this is . . . Pono.
Translation: Do the right thing!

From the Heart,

Thomas L. McGee

Acknowledgments

My special thanks to Cecil Highly of Louisville, KY for bringing this story to life with his wonderful illustrations and cover design. As an artist and a teacher, Cecil has inspired the lives of students and art lovers alike for decades. I would also like to thank Zack Allen of Louisville, Kentucky and Jazmyn Mann of Maui, Hawaii for their help in the development of some of the character illustrations in this book. Both of these talented young people are currently working on special projects of their own.

Many of the characters introduced in this work depict the personalities of actual children on the Island of Maui. There is nothing more inspirational than to look at life afresh through the eyes of a child.

Above all, I thank my dear wife Robin for her loving support and encouragement in the development of the Socrates Adventure series. Happy 37th honey!

Contents

NUIMALU

Chapter 1

Navigating the dimensional corridor felt like a dream trek in slow motion—no propulsion, no control of movement—helplessly tumbling through time and inner space. It took only seconds for the journey to end in a cushioned freefall into an ancient sea. Kaihula wasted no time moving her infants to a staging area where her mate NuiMalu was anxiously awaiting her return. His eyes started glowing with excitement when Kaihula and six newborns swam into view. Socrates and his friends backed away to give the proud parents some privacy. Nui kept the reunion brief because the area was not safe. Acting decisively, he hurried everyone toward the safety of his family's domain. As they sped away,

Poker looked up and saw Shredder cruising near the surface. Pokers anger at the mako exploded and he took off toward the shark in a rage when, out of the dim background came a familiar voice: *"Hey Poker, what's happening?"* Poker stopped so sudden that water rushed past him in a rippling current.

"Jacko, is that you? Oh, dude, you sure had us all worried. How could you let Shredder get you into this mess?"

"I don't know; I guess it was the humiliation of being called a coward in front of Bondar and Two Stars. But hey, what about you, something crazy must have happened to bring you here? Kaihula assured me she would be getting Shredder and me back as soon as her babies arrived. What is going on?"

Nui suddenly shouted in panic, *"Kaihula, take the little ones! All of you follow her! I've got this!"*

Socrates, Poker, and Jacko spun around, their eyes locking onto a frightful image: an enormous reptilian flying creature targeting Shredder. The beast passed over the top of the water twice, then came swooping in low for the kill. Nui sped toward the surface, positioning himself directly under Shredder to avoid detection. Socrates, Poker, and Jacko instinctively followed his lead. The beast timed its kill perfectly and in an instant had Shredder clutched in the grip of its huge, razor sharp talons, plucking him from the water like an eagle snatching a trout from a lake. The creature immediately turned heavenward with wings spread wide and neck extended, gleefully screeching its victory. Its success was short lived: NuiMalu broke the surface at high speed with mouth wide open and, locking the beast's neck in his powerful jaws, came crashing back hard into the water, slashing his head ferociously from side to side while diving straight for the bottom. Poker and Jacko responded by piercing the predator's body through with their swords while Socrates joined in, targeting the top of the talons and biting down hard to get Shredder out of its grip. It took only a moment for the fight to end. The beast was dead, leaving a cut and bleeding Shredder lifelessly floating belly-up. Poker and Jacko once again swung into action, rolling Shredder over and positioning him tightly between them, moving him forward to get oxygen through his gills. Poker called out, "C'mon you toothy goofball, move! You can do it! Do not give up!" Detecting Shredder coming to he continued: "Are those bubbles? Are you doing bubbles? You must be breathing because where else would the bubbles be coming from? Makos sure do have a problem with the bubbles!"

Shredder lazily opened his eyes and in a strained voice said, "Ah, shut up! No, I am not doing bubbles . . . you crazy swordfish!"

Socrates and Jacko started laughing.

Astonished, Nui backed away. He thought the others would have rejoiced at the mako's demise. Instead, they risked their lives to save him and were now working together to revive him. Socrates looked at Nui with a smile and a shrug and said, "Hey, it's called . . . teamwork."

Nui responded by saying, "Well, how about sharing a meal together? " Motioning toward the pterodactyl he urged; "Eat all you can; your next opportunity could take awhile."

Socrates lip curled in defiance of the suggestion, he and his friends backing away from the repulsive carcass, rejecting even the thought actually eating it. Nui continued; "You may think that I am kidding, but we do not joke around much in this place. Food is food no matter what its source. I suggest you take advantage of it before the crocs smell it, and that will not take long."

He quickly began tearing the creature's flesh apart, hastening them to eat their fill.

Chapter 2

The scent of death spread quickly through the region, triggering an automatic response from the plesiosaurs gravest enemies. Detecting their approach, Nui hurried his guests away, leading them to a hidden high ledge to get a clear view of the monsters arriving to feast on the carrion. A wave of fear swept over them at the sight of the gruesome beasts. Resembling saltwater crocodiles, these were massive in comparison, their heads being at least a fourth of their overall body length, their backs lined with thick horizontal rows of curled armor. Scarier still were their jaws, the front of their snouts sporting long, curled back at the tip, glistening fangs followed by multiple rows of triangular, razor sharp teeth. They began ripping apart the avian remains with omnipotent savagery, the entire carcass disappearing in a matter of moments. The crocs then circled, scanning the area in search of more food. They finally swam away, disappearing into their hiding places, silently awaiting another victim.

Once the area appeared safe, Poker raced forward with a defiant look and said, "Let me at 'em, let me at 'em!"

Nui was stunned and hustled to pull Poker back to the ledge. Socrates, Jacko, and Shredder watched Nui, wondering how long it would take him to *get it*. Nevertheless, they could not hold in their urge to laugh very long and suddenly busted out in hysterics. Nui finally managed to figure out Poker's improvisation, rolled his eyes, and started chuckling. Addressing Poker, Nui asked, "What is with you? At first, you are angry with your friend, then you help save him, and now you turn a horror story into comedy. Are you nuts?"

Poker crossed his eyes, cocked his head to one side, and said, *"Say whaaat?"*

Nui totally lost it. He was laughing so hard that he could not speak, swim, or even move. It was a good thing that their location was secret because none of them was currently in any condition to be serious about another fight. Regaining his composure, Nui warned; "Look, guys, you are going to have to keep your zany remarks to a minimum. Your lives require being on constant alert and one small mistake could result in a battle to the death. And believe me; in this place, each of you is very close to the bottom of the food chain."

Chapter 3

Nui led the four away to the security of his family's hidden sanctuary and, seeing his family intact, gave way to a sigh of relief. Sensing Nui and Kaihula's need for some private time with their babies, Kaihula's parents, Mau and Makana, offered a guided tour to the newcomers.

Leading them some distance away, Mau began his oration: "The interior of our cavern is thousands of feet deep, while the entrance fronts an enormous bay. Krill and baitfish are abundant here and we have no problem protecting our food supply from other species competing for it. That is of course, with the exception of a large number of evil humans living in the rock masses above the bay and the pterodactyls, one of which you confronted earlier. Together they pose a slight risk to our food source. However, we have managed with some scare tactics to limit their desire for a chance confrontation with us. As peaceful as we try to be, our family has no problem playing the role of '*terrifying-nasties*' when it comes to protecting what is ours."

Mau and Makana continued the tour, spending a significant amount of time pointing out the highlights and dangers of their domain. Upon returning to the privacy of the plesiosaurs secret place, NuiMalu quickly greeted them, thanking Socrates and his pals and for what they had done to save his family: "You risked your lives and your futures in your beautiful kingdom to save someone you don't even know."

Amaya answered; "Were we wrong to trust you?"

"Well, no," Nui responded, "but how could you tell we were worth your trust?"

Two Stars swam up alongside Amaya and in a soft voice responded to Nui; "A mother that risks everything for her young deserves trust. Seeing Kaihula for the first time with little Manny was the most incredible display of affection we have ever seen. Others cannot help but be drawn to someone like that. Now that we are acquainted, I would have to say that our instincts have been right on, wouldn't you agree?"

Kaihula and Makana swam over to Amaya, Two Stars, Auntie Noni, Serine, and Zippee, kindly rubbing their faces against them. Kaihula softly whispered; "You are more than we deserve."

Socrates, once again brimming with curiosity, questioned Mau and Nui: "So, why does Kaihula take the risk of laying her eggs on the other side of the dimensional window?"

Mau's eyes slumped in silent reflection, a look of grief seizing his countenance. He then began his explanation: "Many generations ago, an epoch event happened that completely changed the world. A giant fiery object struck the ocean, lighting it up with the brilliance of a thousand suns, and sending a devastating shock wave circling the world. Tearing landmasses from their foundations, the vicious currents re-arranged everything previously known before the agitation subsided. Every creature felt its affect in some way, the majority perishing. Those of us who typically make our home in the deep, obscure trenches of the ocean floor fared best. However, the *'event'* changed life as we knew it."

Mau shortly hesitated.

"What do you mean . . . what changed," asked Socrates?

"On the positive side, those of us trapped under the blanket of the object's melted expanse benefit immensely from the incredibly pure water. On the other hand, we never again saw the sky. The light we enjoy is mysteriously constant; which is strange being that no luminaries are visible. The object actually created a world within itself, altering our lives in a significant way."

Mau's eyes glared into the distance for a moment. He then turned to Socrates and said; "*Time*—is trapped here. None of us—age."

Socrates replied; "That's a good thing, right?"

"Yes, you could say that. Only, there is a serious downside. Some of the creatures trapped here are of the deadliest species the world has ever seen. The upside is that, with the change to our environment, most are . . . hybrid. Nothing except plants, small fish, and extreme deep-water species like ourselves, can successfully reproduce. The numbers of most ancient species slowly continues to dwindle, your earlier fight with the pterodactyl being one of the causes. The good thing for our family is that one more horrifying vestige of the past is now history. Unfortunately, every day brings another challenge to our survival. For instance: when Kaihula and Makana begin laying their eggs, oxygen rich, silvery bubbles start emitting from the eggs shells until the infants hatch. The off gassing draws a lot of attention to the location of their nests. That is why we use the dimensional window when it comes time to spawn our young. The isolated area of their nests on the other side remains completely devoid of any danger to their eggs development."

Uncle Gnarls questioned Mau; "If you have that figured out, and your species has lived from the indefinite past, why are there not more of you?"

Nui answered; "Sadly, some of our young have fallen prey to the crocs on our return through the window. The impulsiveness of our newborns puts them in perilous situations. Others have simply disappeared through small spaces deep within our cavern. We have no idea what has happened to them because the openings are too small for us adults to navigate through to see where they ended up and no doubt, they are now too large to return. For the first time *ever* . . . we have managed to get *all* our newborns back safely, thanks to the actions of you and your friends. We are deeply indebted to you."

"You don't have to be," stated Uncle Gnarls. "The way we see it is that we have an obligation to help each other regardless of the risks."

Nui took a moment, looking each of Socrates' friends in their eyes, acknowledging; "You certainly proved that today. Only, our gravest problem we have yet to show you. All other dangers fade in comparison."

Nui led everyone to where the cavern fronts the enormous bay. None of them was in any way prepared for what they would see from another of Nui's secret lookouts.

Humans, large muscular humans, were encamped on a land mass at the end of the bay. Nui elaborated on what Mau had touched on earlier: "This whole region, including the area you arrived from, was part of their kingdom. They are evil creatures from the distant past that built an island mecca in the middle of the sea. They are the ones who designed the large crystal to harness the suns energy during a solar event, dispersing intense light through their network of caverns, causing the ocean to appear to dance with golden fire, for no other reason I suppose than to show off their magnificence. Most perished ages ago, when what we call . . . 'the flaming star' . . . hit this region. Yet, some of them happened to be within the far reaches of this bay and were able to survive: only now, they too remain trapped. What these do not know is that the crystal's energy created a passage that connects your world with ours. Surprisingly, the canyon where the crystal is located sustained no real damage from the cosmic event even though a powerful force remains within the canyons structure, having caused some major catastrophes over the years. Mau and Makana discovered the strange passage you arrived through a long time ago. Mau approached the quivering mass, drawn by its mysterious presence in the middle of a wall of stone. Cautiously nudging up against it, he disappeared. Makana went in after him. They ended up in the cavern where all of you were before coming here. Kaihula and I used to explore it with them frequently. We felt fortunate to have finally discovered an area where Kaihula and Makanas' eggs can safely hatch, far away from the ever-present danger we experience on this side. Our hope is that we can keep this brood of young ones subdued in our protected area long enough for them to grow up."

Kaihula swam in close to her mate, "Honey, perhaps you should show them, you know . . . the other problem we have in the bay."

Nui agreed and led the way to another location. Socrates was in shock by what he saw and heard. Overpowering masters were forcing humans of smaller stature to harvest sea plants and construct huge dwellings, frequently beating their captives mercilessly to keep them moving. Screams of the unfortunate echoed throughout the bay, making Socrates feel sick, he sorrowing at their demise of not being able to escape . . . even into the sleep of death. Once again, Socrates' demeanor changed from puzzlement to anger, knowing that this situation too, had to be changed.

It was time to return to Nui's cavern to come up with a plan.

CAPTAIN SAM O'BRIEN

Chapter 4

Sam O'Brien, the cruise ship skipper of the near ill-fated 'Ocean Gem,' was sitting in his stateroom reviewing the ships log of the perilous event he recently experienced in the Bermuda Triangle. Suddenly, Corey Coulson, one of his crewmembers, interrupted him: "Captain, the parents of young Tooney, you know, the little boy we saved on our last cruise, are here to see you sir."

"What do you mean the boy *we* saved; you mean the boy the *dolphin* saved, don't you?"

"Sorry sir, yes sir, including a host of other fish from my perspective."

The Captain smiled; "Quick, show them in Seaman Coulson, and please, arrange for some liquid refreshment."

Tooney's parents were excited to be re-uniting with the man who, guided by no more than gut instinct, common sense, and a willingness to listen, helped save their son.

"Charlie, Carlynn, come on in. What a pleasure it is to see you two. You both look good. By the way, the owners of the Ocean Gem have agreed to give everyone who was on board our cruise a complimentary, two-week excursion to Hawaii. You can go anytime you like. Of course, you and Tooney are to have a luxury suite and will be dining at my table every day. The press coverage of our trip has everyone excited and we are completely booked for the entire season."

"Thank you Captain," Charlie replied, "that is certainly gracious of your employers. However, my wife and I are puzzled over something Tooney has been repeating for the past several days. It has something to do with a crystal. We thought that maybe you could help us figure out what he is trying to say. It seems connected to his experience with the dolphin. Would you mind seeing him for a moment?"

The Captain lit up when he realized that Tooney was waiting right outside the door hand in hand with his grandmother, one of the only people the little boy trusted. "Please, bring him in," the Captain responded, "I cannot wait to see him."

Carlynn opened the door, motioning her mother to bring Tooney inside the room. Realizing how delicate the emotions of a child with Tooney's introversion can be, the Captain restrained his urge to whisk him up in his arms and hug him. In a tender voice the Captain said, "Welcome to my quarters Tooney. Would you like a cold soda?"

Forcing a slight smile, Tooney nodded affirmatively. His father asked; "Son, would you prefer to be alone with the Captain?"

For a moment, Tooney did not answer. Gazing at all the nautical décor, he slowly made his way around the room, gently touching each item. His parents and grandmother silently slipped out the door. Once realizing that he and the Captain were alone, Tooney finally managed a glancing eye contact.

The Captain initiated the conversation: "So young man, your parents shared with me your interest in a crystal. Would you like to tell me about it?"

Tooney, reacting to a nautical map on the Captain's wall, walked over and briefly scanned the beautifully diagrammed overview of the world and its oceans. In only a matter of seconds, he pointed to a particular spot in the Atlantic Ocean and said forcefully, "Right there; water crystal is right there!"

The Captain was impressed at how quickly Tooney pointed out the area where their ship almost went down. He asked, "What do you mean? Did you see something when you were with the dolphin?"

The little boy grinned from ear to ear at the mention of the young dolphin that helped save him. Tooney pointed again to the same spot on the map, and in an even more determined tone stated; "Right there; water crystal is right there!"

This time the Captain detected the need to calm Tooney and suggested, "Well, why don't the two of us go out there and check it out."

The Captain moved closer to the map, focusing intently at the spot Tooney was pointing to and asked, "Do you have any idea why it's there?"

"Crystal opens *window!*"

The Captain asked, "What window?"

"*Cavern* window," came the reply.

The Captain's eyes narrowed: "Did the dolphin take you into a cavern?"

The little boys face beamed with excitement, responding; "Dolphin took Tooney into *canyon* with crystal and *golden cavern* with shiny window. Water window is pretty and wavy, but Tooney's arm did not get wet."

At this point, the Captain was completely baffled. He sensed that Tooney was possibly holding the key to a major discovery, something he was going to need help with and that would require a high level of confidentiality. He wondered; "Who can we trust?" Two names came to mind.

The Captain gently held out both his hands and kneeled down in front of Tooney. The shy little boy responded by placing his hands on the Captain's. The Captain whispered; "For now, Tooney, we have to keep this a secret until we can find someone we can trust to help us. Are you okay with keeping this a secret?"

With eyes shining, Tooney looked at the Captain and said, "I like a secret. Can Tooney and Captain work on secret today?"

"I tell you what; you go and get some rest tonight while I make some phone calls and we'll get started in the morning. However," the Captain hesitated while taking a roll out of a cardboard tube, "I received this new map today; it highlights the area where our ship got into trouble and I would appreciate your looking it over tonight. Would you do that for me? It will speed up our search."

Tooney was ecstatic. He took the map, ran to the door, threw it open, and called out to his dad, "Quick, papa, gotta' go!"

Charlie curiously glanced at the Captain as he passed the open door to his quarters. Sam O'Brien winked at Charlie and said, "Bring him back tomorrow morning at 7:30. Oh, and by the way—examine the map with him tonight."

Chapter 5

The Captain immediately thought of two old Navy friends who had previously worked with him in special discovery operations. Though he had seen neither of them for many years, he felt confident that they would jump at the chance to explore what was now unfolding as another Bermuda Triangle mystery. No sooner had Tooney's parents exited the ship than the Captain picked up the phone and dialed the number of his old friend, retired Admiral, George McCauley. The phone picked up after only two rings: "Admiral McCauley's office; Lieutenant Christopher speaking."

"Yes, this is Captain Sam O'Brien. I would like to speak with Admiral McCauley please."

"I am sorry sir; Admiral McCauley is in a meeting and cannot be disturbed. May I have him call you later in the day?"

Sam, in a very stern tone replied, "Please, just tell him who is calling and that it is about a significant matter. Oh, and Lieutenant, make sure we have a secure line."

The Lieutenant sighed and took a chance, putting Sam on hold while paging the Admiral: "Admiral, you have an important call sir."

"Look, Lieutenant, I told you to hold my calls! Take a message and I will call them back later!"

"Sorry sir, but the call is from Captain Sam O'Brien."

"Well, why didn't you say so? Put him on the intercom."

"He requested a secure line sir."

"Okay, I guess we can break for a moment." After dismissing his staff, he picked up the phone: "Sam . . . how is my old friend? I saw the news report of your little mishap in the triangle. Tell me, were you wearing your brown pants?"

Sam responded, "Oh, you are so-o-o funny."

The Admiral chuckled, then asked; "What has you calling me on a secure line? Are you in trouble with your company?"

"Far from it: At the moment I seem to be the most sought after skipper in the cruise industry. Our experience in the Triangle has launched us to the top of popularity as the safest ship afloat. I am not sure we deserve all the praise, but the company's bottom-line sure looks good. The reason I called is that—I need your help with a map. Could you make some time? It won't take long."

"Where are you?"

"Currently, at Cape Hatteras; our ship is in dry dock for two weeks pending a damage assessment."

"Well, for crying out loud. I am at our old facility not more than fifteen minutes from the docks. Do you remember how to get here?"

"How can I forget? It is still hard to get over the disappointment of the government cutting our funding just prior to launching the submersible. You are not still working on our idea are you?"

"Well, yes and no. The feds recently decided to resume the funding . . . once I agreed to a compromise."

"I don't get it: with the world in such a desperate plight, what could have possibly re-sparked their interest in isopod exploration?"

"That is something I cannot discuss over the phone. You are welcome to stop by though; maybe we can help each other."

"How is tomorrow at 0800 hours?"

"You got it."

Chapter 6

Arriving at the covert facility, Sam checked in with security, following the necessary protocol required to gain access to the meeting. The Admiral was excited to see him: "Sam, come on in."

Captain O'Brien entered the room with Tooney at his side. At least two dozen military officers were sitting around an enormous table along with several scientists who were busy working on solving an equation presented on a green board that was easily twenty feet across and five feet high. The presentation of symbols, numbers, and atomic structure, far surpassed Captain O'Brien's knowledge of scientific theory.

The Admiral continued; "Please, take a seat; we are working on something that might grab your interest. By the way, who do have tagging along?"

"Admiral, I would like to introduce you to the most intriguing young man I have had the pleasure of cruising with for many years. This is Tooney. You might have heard about him on the news. It was his personal interaction with a young dolphin, and a host of other fish, that helped save our ship."

Everyone in the room started snickering, imagining that Sam was over embellishing the story to make young Tooney feel special. The Captain was not amused. In an irritated tone of voice he stated; "Look, maybe we have come at a bad time. You all seem so preoccupied with your project that perhaps another day would be better."

The Admiral responded, "No, Sam, hold on. The media coverage of your ship's experience in the Triangle does seem a bit theatrical, that is all. We would certainly welcome some firsthand clarification. Please, sit down. Your input could be valuable to us."

Reluctantly, the Captain and Tooney took a seat. Glancing at the almost mile long equation presented on the green board, Tooney instantly comprehended the mistakes and quickly covered his mouth with his hands, stifling his urge to laugh. Just then, another man, dressed in a black robe and white collar, entered the room.

"Sam," said the Admiral, "I would like you to meet Father Schanessey. Father, this is my old friend, Captain Sam O'Brien."

The priest looked as if he had seen a ghost. The Captain looked deep into the bearded operates eyes with suspicion and did not hold out his hand in greeting.

The Admiral sensed friction between the men and said, "Come on you two, let's get down to business?"

While taking his seat, the priest noticed young Tooney and winked at him. Tooney hid his face behind the Captain.

Sam asked, "Okay admiral, why did you have us come *here*? Just what are you working on?"

"To tell you the truth, we are only a heartbeat away from something that will give our country ultimate military superiority over the seas for at least the next hundred years. Are you interested?"

The Captain grimaced; "This is a *military* operation—and you need a *priest?*"

"Hey, you know how it is; a little prayer never hurts. All the bases have to be covered, right?"

Captain O'Brien's countenance turned instantly into anger. "So that's it; everything you are working on is for military superiority! What has happened to you George? We had a pact to focus on ways to help mankind, not to impede his progress; especially by wasting time on worthless one-upmanship!"

"Yeah, Sam, but that was before the world got turned upside down with terrorism!"

Sam stood up, looking stone cold at the priest, and answered; "It seems to me that the world got turned upside down with terrorism during the *crusades!*" He then scornfully fired a verbal reproof to the entire group in attendance: "The one basic thing each of you should have learned from history is recognizing the need for ridding yourselves of the *core* of this world's chaos, the number one *cause* of young lives and valuable resources being wasted on military campaigns!" Sternly pointing his finger at the priest he concluded; "It seems to me that the real enemy . . . is the worldwide systems of hypocritical religion that continue to divide people, needlessly keeping the nations at each other's throat!" Grabbing Tooney by the hand he said, "Let's go, I have obviously made a *poor choice.*"

The Admiral was furious: "Oh that is just great Sam! I give you some of my valuable time, and you come in here insulting me, judging me before my men!"

"From my perspective, Admiral, that judgment is in the hands of someone far greater than me."

Disappointed and disgusted, Captain O'Brien simply dismissed himself and young Tooney by saying: "Good day, gentlemen!"

Chapter 7

Sam was driving fast to get back to the ship, being frustrated out of his mind over the Admiral's apparent disregard for their solemn promise to avoid any further military pursuits with the exception of assisting in peaceful exploration. He finally turned to Tooney, who could not stop giggling, and asked in a disturbed tone of voice; "Is something funny?"

"Yes, funny," replied Tooney, "we hit two birds with same rock."

"What are you are talking about?"

"Go to Captain's quarters; Tooney wants to draw."

The Captain had no idea what was going through this young man's mind, but was certainly eager to find out.

Back in the privacy of his quarters the Captain asked Tooney; "All right, before you do any drawing, what is it you have figured out?"

"Priest not Father Schanessey; His name—Edmund Tucker, alias Father Dominic Kabinsky, from Boston."

The name Kabinsky caused the Captain's hair to stand up on the back of his neck, sending cold chills racing through his body. He immediately summoned Tooney's parents.

Charlie sensed Sam's alarm: "Is everything okay? I came as quickly as I could."

"Yes, Charlie, everything is fine. It is just that your son identified a fugitive priest this morning whose capture is going to turn the religious community in this country on its ear. You had better get Carlynn in here because there is going to be a fire storm."

"I am sorry Captain: We should have forewarned you about Tooney's special interests. Aside from his infatuation with science and animals, he reads every police blog on unsolved felonies nationwide. He probably has logged in his memory every case in this country for the past twenty years. He can literally pick a needle out of a haystack."

The Captain had Charlie and Carlynn take a seat, giving them a brief overview of the priests' crimes and his subsequent conviction and escape. He wrapped up the conversation by saying, "Justice is finally going to be served."

The immediate situation was delicate and Sam did not want Charlie's family put at risk, so he turned them over to the capable hands of his staff, making special arrangements for their safety in a suite on the ship reserved only for political dignitaries.

The Captain then made a call to an FBI field office in Boston: "Give me James Powell please."

"May I ask who is calling?"

"Yes, this is Captain Sam O'Brien."

The phone picked up in only a second; "*Sam*, how have you been? My staff has been following the news reports about your narrow escape in the Triangle. We are so glad that your ship made it out safe. You have got to fill me in on the story sometime."

"Believe me James; I cannot wait to share all the details with you. However, for now, I need your help putting to rest a fifteen year old case concerning a convicted priest who managed to escape after being sentenced for a crime involving my nephew, as well as a multitude of other children."

For a moment, the line went silent: "Don't tell me you have found that pervert?"

"We have not only found him, but, get this . . . he is working for the government. I think it is high time he has another go round with the justice department; what do you say?"

"Where are you Sam?"

"We are in dry dock at Cape Hatteras. My ship is the 'Ocean Gem'."

"I can be there in three hours. I sure hope that jerk doesn't slip through our fingers again."

Prior to boarding his plane, Agent Powell began rallying the bureau assigned to the Cape for necessary resources, including a troop of military police to bar any attempt by the priest to escape.

A fleet of five, black SUVs pulling into the shipyard ignited a fire of vengeance within Sam O'Brien, his emotions hackling up like a warrior going into battle. Following James' explicit direction, Sam redialed the Admiral's number, getting right to the point: "Look George, I am sorry for my behavior earlier today. I have been through a lot lately and am having a hard time processing what happened in the Triangle. Would you mind if we try again?"

After some tense seconds, the Admiral responded in a stern tone: "Sam, don't trifle with me! I am a busy man! If you need something, ask, but don't waste my time!"

"Understood, Admiral; would you happen to have a few minutes, say, right now?"

"I can spare only about five."

The Admiral's staff had just begun exiting for a break, when the hallway outside their meeting room swarmed with armed men, subduing the priest in a matter of seconds.

Agent Powell entered the hallway with Captain O'Brien at his side, addressing the criminal impostor: "Father Schanessey, or should I say, Edmund Tucker; how about . . . Father Dominic Kabinsky? You sir are under arrest for felony escape! Oh, and by the way, did you really think that a little age and a beard could forever conceal your pathetic identity from the smartest young man in our country?"

Tooney appeared from behind Captain O'Brien with a half-smile on his face.

The arrogant priest shouted; "Are you going to take that little ret . . . "

Reacting in a blind rage, Captain O'Brien grabbed the man by his collar and spun him around, viciously ramming his head into a wall, breaking his nose. After body slamming him onto the floor, Sam grabbed a hand full of hair, jerking the man's head back as if to break his neck and shouted in his face: "If you try and finish that sentence you will be going to prison in an *ambulance!* Moreover, believe me when I tell you that this is the last little boy you will *ever see!*" Sam then picked him up by the seat of his pants, hurling the bleeding man across the hall into the clutches of a half dozen agents who whisked him outside to a waiting vehicle.

Hearing the commotion, the Admiral came running out of his office just in time to see the agents leading the priest away. *"Sam,"* he demanded, *"what is the meaning of this?"*

"Admiral, your choice of prayer representation did you absolutely no good! Have you become so blind that you could not conduct a simple background check, even for a so-called, *priest*? You know as well as I do the depth of corruption in the church, always turning a blind eye and shuffling this trash around! I really cannot imagine God listening to any request uttered by a convicted *child molester*, much less help you with *military pursuits!* You seriously need to reconsider the principles we agreed to live by all those years ago! Good day, sir!"

The Admiral stood in humiliated silence while Agent Powell's men exited the building.

The Captain, breathing a sigh of relief, apologized to James; "Sorry, I got a little carried away."

Agent Powell replied, "No problem, Sam. If it had been my nephew, I probably would have done far worse. There is one thing about it; he will never again see the light of day. We are sending him directly to our new, privately funded, high-security prison located in Nevada. The facility specializes in . . . surgically managing sexual perversion. It is what the Agency calls . . . justice. I suggest contacting your sister right away. Your family could certainly use some closure. I also think it would be a good idea for them to meet Tooney. After all, he is the hero in all of this."

"Maybe taking them on a cruise would help, huh?"

Agent Powell chuckled; "I personally cannot think of a better plan. Here, take my card. My cell number is on it, in case you need any further help."

Chapter 8

Back at the ship, Captain O'Brien finished wrapping up his earlier conversation with Tooney's parents; "After the priest escaped, my sister and nephew would rarely go out in public due to the humiliation caused by the church's defense attorneys. They tried to pin the blame for the priest's misconduct on the abused children and their families, claiming they were all in on some sort of conspiracy. Then, to top it off, my dear wife passed away from a bought with breast cancer right after our only child was born. Life has been challenging ever since. However, my daughter Chloe and I seem to make due. I will have to introduce you to her. She usually accompanies me aboard ship, attending a school for children of staff members. She recently took a break to visit some of her cousins and will be returning sometime within the next few days. I will call you when she arrives and we will have dinner. How does that sound?"

Charlie replied, "That sounds great Captain; but aren't you forgetting something?"

The Captain looked puzzled, then suddenly realized what he and Tooney had set off to accomplish in the first place; they needed help with the map. He remembered Tooney saying something about taking down two birds with the same rock; what was that all about?

During the Captain's long conversation with Charlie and Carlynn, Tooney had no problem keeping busy. Using a notebook given him by the Captain, and from raw memory, he wrote out the entire equation he had seen on the Admiral's green-board.

The Captain approached him; "Hey, what are you up to young man?" He gasped when Tooney handed him the notebook.

Tooney giggled and said, "Idea good, equation wrong."

The Captain glanced over at Tooney's parents who just shrugged, Charlie saying, "His mind is like a high speed computer; there is not much that gets by him."

Sam O'Brien had known some amazing people in his life; however, nothing he had ever experienced could have prepared him for the talents of young Tooney. He felt he was in the presence of Albert Einstein, Sherlock Holmes, and Sir Isaac Newton all rolled into one super-human personality. He hesitated to ask Tooney anything further, feeling it would be best to seek the help of someone familiar with this degree of complex theory before pressing for an answer he could not understand anyway. It was a long shot trying to contact his old shipmate Buddy Gold. They had served a stint in the Navy together, only their communication had been limited over the years. Yet, after his disappointment with the Admiral, Sam felt Buddy was the only other person he could trust with Tooney's discovery. What was more; Buddy had worked not only with NASA on aeronautics technologies but also with the Navy as a private contractor developing deep-water submersibles. He was also an avid student of the Atlantic's ocean-floor topography. The problem would be . . . finding him. Sam smiled with an idea. After politely concluding his conversation with Tooney's parents and seeing them off for the day, he picked up the phone and dialed Agent Powell's private line:

"This is Agent Powell."

"James, this is Sam."

"Hey, old friend, long time no see. What has it been, three . . . maybe . . . four hours?"

They both chuckled for a moment; "James, I have a favor to ask: I am working on something highly confidential and need help finding an old friend. His name is Buddy Gold. Is it possible that you could help me find him? What I know is that the last I talked to him, he was somewhere in Maine working on sea-scape imagery."

"Captain, what you and Tooney have just done for the Agency puts us at your disposal. Only, I am curious as to what you are up to."

"I will fill you in soon. I have to get some clarification on something Tooney has discovered before I can share any information."

"Understood; we'll get right on it."

Chapter 9

That evening, after settling in, the Captain was recapping the day's events when his phone rang: "This is Captain O'Brien."

"Sam, this is Buddy Gold."

"Buddy, it is sure good to hear your voice. Agent Powell obviously got a hold of you, huh?"

"Well, yeah, and when he said he was from the FBI, I thought I was in some sort of trouble. With all the classified information I have locked in my head, I have to hide out just to keep the wolf from the door, if you know what I mean. So, what is it that is so important?"

"Are you ready for a wild ride? Because a friend and me have stumbled on to something that is going to make anything you have ever worked on look like a game of marbles. If you are interested we could sure use your help."

"Where are you right now, Sam?"

"We are in dry dock at Cape Hatteras. My ship is the 'Ocean Gem'."

"I can be there tomorrow morning at say, nine a.m."

"Where will you be coming in from?"

"That's also classified. Don't ask."

The following morning was beautiful, with sea birds squawking and swooping all around the docks while excited anglers were firing up their engines, preparing to head out for a promising day of fishing. The electricity in the air reminded Sam of the races at Daytona where the rays of the early morning sun and the roar of supercharged exhaust gets your adrenaline pumping, sending shivers up your spine. The Captain and Tooney stationed themselves at the head of the gangplank, anxiously awaiting Buddy's arrival. At nine o'clock sharp, a taxi pulled up and Buddy stepped out. He looked a bit weathered since Sam had seen him last, yet, he was surprisingly fit.

While boarding the ship, Buddy looked up and smiled, "Sam, look at you, you look great. How long has it been, fifteen, maybe seventeen years?"

"It has been quite a while; you don't look so bad yourself. I half-way expected you to have lost most of your hair by now. You're not involved in some sort of genetic experiment are you?"

Buddy smirked, "Nice; who is your sidekick there?"

"This is Tooney; you might recognize him from the media coverage of our close call in the Triangle."

"Ah, Tooney, yes . . . I have seen pictures of you and your parents in the news. I believe you are probably the most inspirational young person in our country right now."

Tooney smiled, but could not manage eye contact; he just kept glancing around at his surroundings. Detecting the boy's shyness, Buddy attempted a friendly gesture, gently holding out his hand, giving an opportunity to respond. Tooney finally managed a slight hand-tap.

"So, Tooney, now that we have been officially introduced, maybe you and Sam can fill me in on what you have discovered."

Sam replied, "Let's go to my quarters and we can get started."

As soon as the three entered the room, Tooney briefly looked up at the Captain who motioned with his eyes towards the little boys writing tablet. Tooney excitedly retrieved the tablet from the Sam's desk and sat down in a chair. The Captain and Buddy walked over and began staring at the incredible scientific formula that Tooney had previously written out. Immediately recognizing the formula, Buddy's eyes opened wide; "No," he blurted out, "not possible! Where did this come from?"

Sam replied, "From a military meeting with our old friend Admiral George McCauley. He and an elite staff of advisors were working on it. They had it written out on a huge green board in their secret meeting room. I really did not pay much attention to it but the Admiral did suggest that what they were working on could provide this country with ultimate military superiority over our world's oceans for the next century."

"Okay," Buddy replied in a panic, "but how did you manage to copy the formula on this tablet? They certainly wouldn't let you just . . . *jot it down!*"

Tooney smiled while the Captain responded: "Well, that is where Tooney comes in. He memorized it while we were in the Admirals office and wrote it out when we arrived back here."

"And just how long were you in the Admirals office?"

"Oh, not more than say, two, maybe three minutes."

Buddy appeared in a state of shock. "Sam, military scientists have been mulling over this particular formula for at least twenty years and, to date, no one has been able to unravel its flaws. It is an attempt to unlock the secrets of an element that can be used in aquatic stealth technologies."

Buddy walked around from the back of Tooney's chair and stared down at the little boy saying, "Tooney, would you mind if I hold your tablet for just a minute?"

Tooney quickly shuffled the tablet out of his lap and into Buddy's hands, once again, giggling.

Buddy looked at him and asked, "Is something funny?"

Tooney reached out and, taking the tablet back, walked over to the Captain's desk and started writing the formula out again on a clean page, this time with the mistakes corrected. Buddy and Sam stared over his shoulders, both dumbfounded at how quickly the little boy was able to complete his task.

When finished, he handed the tablet back to Buddy and said, "There, that will work."

Buddy's jaw dropped, his face turning pale. Plopping down in a chair, his trembling hands were holding the formula in one hand and his slumped-over head in the other. Sam hurried to his side and asked, "Buddy, are you okay?"

After a brief silence, Buddy started laughing. Looking up at Tooney he said, "You, young man, are amazing. No, you are more than amazing: you are incredible. How did you do this?"

Tooney explained, "All matter follows an atomic pattern. The dynamic is simple when turning it inside out."

Neither Sam nor Buddy had any idea what Tooney meant by that statement. However, Buddy was certainly aware of what this discovery could mean for the scientific community; especially those interested in deep water exploration. Sam finally blurted out; "I cannot stand it anymore! What is the formula for?"

Buddy extended his arm with an open hand, inviting Tooney, "Do you want to tell him, or should I?"

Responding to the Captain's burning curiosity, Tooney replied, "Transparent Titanium."

Sam winced, closing his eyes while absorbing Tooney's answer, finally asking, "Depth to pressure ratios?"

Buddys' reply: "With a correct hull design, it is more than satisfactory for any depths in our world's oceans."

They both glanced over at Tooney who had sat back down, repeating his exercise of writing out the formula. Three quarters of the way through he stopped, made a change, and stated, "Maybe this one would be better."

Both men raced over to see what he had changed. Buddy dropped to his knees, staring at the revision in disbelief, asking, "Are you sure?"

Tooney nodded his head affirmatively.

Sam asked, "What, what has changed?"

Buddy stood back up, addressing Sam with a big smile on his face; "Tell me, your martinis, how do you prefer them; wet or dry?"

Sam looked at him as if he were crazy. However, after a moment of contemplating Buddy's inference, Sam's eyes rolled in wonder: "No, that is not possible!"

"It is not only possible, but this cool-gel form makes it manageable in any shape you desire, completely unaffected by any depth or pressure. Yes my friend, good old clear, liquid titanium; you cannot beat it." He then began strolling around the room, laughing hysterically, adding; "My entire adult life has been spent pursuing better technologies for marine and space science. In all of those years, it is amazing how many have hypothesized on something like this, their formulas inevitably dismissed and always ending up in the trash. Then along comes young Tooney . . . who writes this out like a simple dinner menu."

A pause of quiet reflection followed with Buddy's eyes fixated on the formula, his mind racing with technological possibilities as to the titanium's use. Within moments though, his countenance changed, a wave of fear gripping him. He blurted out; "We have to keep this a secret! The ramifications could be lethal to the planet if it falls into the wrong hands!"

Tooney, who had been silently strolling around the room, walked over and tugged at the Captain's jacket.

The Captain responded, "What is it Tooney?"

"Can we explore the canyon and cavern now?"

Sam, with a slightly embarrassed look on his face turned to Buddy and said, "We have something far more important to discuss with you."

Buddy's eyes rolled sideways, then up; "You are kidding, right? What could be more important than what we have just discovered?"

Sam instructed Tooney, "Go over to the map and point to where the cavern is."

Hurrying across the room, the youngster put his finger on a specific place on the map; "Cavern is right there!"

Buddy asked, "What cavern?"

"Tooney claims it is a gold-lined cavern with huge ancient statues; you know . . . half man-half fish images. There seems to be some sort of window in the cavern that shimmers like water, only, Tooney said it was not wet when he pushed his hand into it."

Tooney added; "Tell about canyon with crystal."

By now, the Captain was reluctant to say another word.

Buddy spread his arms out wide, his fingers contracting, silently urging Sam to explain.

"I was going to get to that; only, I was not the one who saw all of what we are talking about. I was busy trying to get our ship out of the grip of something trying to drag us down while my crew was pulling panicked passengers from the water. The . . . uh . . . fish were bringing them to the side."

Buddy threw his hands in the air to stop the conversation: "*Hold it . . . Time out*! What do you mean by fish bringing people to the side? What kind of fish?"

Considering Buddy's perception of this conversation, Sam awkwardly replied: "Oh, you know, the average run of the mill life-saving fish like . . . dolphins, um . . . hammerheads, and uh . . . makos. Actually, the people in the water resembled a lunch-line for hungry sharks. Yet, not one person came out of the water harmed in any way. Moreover, when everyone was back on board safe, swordfish and barracuda by the hundreds began leaping out of the water as if they were—making some sort of statement."

Buddy sighed, "Something tells me there is more to this story?"

The Captain was feeling embarrassed by this ridiculous dialogue and began stammering, his voice racing, realizing how foolish all of this sounded: "A-a-a—and that is where

Tooney comes in. It just s-s-so happens that when we pulled away from the trouble spot and did our census of everyone on-board; we found he was the only one missing. A young dolphin evidently kept him in a safe place until we could return to look for him. The water was actually swarming with fish guiding us to the particular spot where we found him. Buddy, I know all of this sounds crazy, but the area is definitely worth exploring. What do you say; are you up for a *crazy* adventure? It might be our opportunity to uncover the *source* of all the phenomena in the Triangle."

Buddy said nothing for at least the next five minutes, all the while pacing back and forth across the room, his head shifting from side to side, staring hard at the specific place Tooney had pointed out on the map. He could not help thinking of the media coverage of the Ocean Gem's mishap in the Bermuda Triangle along with the reported testimonies of hundreds of the ship's passengers. There had to be something to this story, the mystery of it intriguing him. He finally stopped, took a deep breath, turned to Sam and Tooney and said; "Okay, I'm in. However, start over from the beginning and—*slow down*. I need to hear every detail of your cruise from beginning to end, including what has happened since your return to port."

BIG JAKE

BAAYA

JAZZY

Chapter 10

Bondar had been stressing for days. He was the hammerhead shark that was the last to see Socrates and his friends as they leaped through the dimensional window in order to rescue Kaihula's newborns. Big Jake and several other humpback whales, along with teams of hammerheads, makos, barracuda, dolphins, and swordfish were also staying close to the area of the disappearance. Daily, Bondar would swim into the cavern, recounting the events leading up to that final moment and staring at the dark wall of stone, feeling sickened over his inability to do anything that could help get his friends back. On one particular evening, he finally gave in to some serious conversation with Big Jake.

"Look Bondar," Big Jake began, "you tried everything you could to help. You have to lighten up a bit. Socrates and Two Stars will get this thing figured out. And when they do, we will all be here, ready to help in any way we can."

"Thanks, Jake; I really appreciate your hanging around. I just cannot get out of my mind what Two Stars said about the place where Kaihula lives; she said it was a 'dimension of terror'. What did she mean by that? After all, what could be more terrifying than us; you know what I mean?"

Jake started snickering and said, "Yeah, you are pretty ugly."

"I wouldn't be talking . . . you knobby-headed doofus."

They gave each other a cold stare and then—started cracking up.

"Hey," said Jake, "these are beauty spots I'll have you know."

"Oh, I'm sorry," came back Bondar, "I just heard some of your pals call you a knot-head and assumed they were describing your appearance."

"Yeah, well, at least my eyes are still attached to my mainframe."

They both grew silent for another moment . . . and then broke out in laughter again.

"Oh, what the heck," said Bondar, "Let's go check on everyone back at the reef."

"Good idea."

A short distance from the north end of the canyon Bondar noticed one of the most unusual things he had ever seen. A young female tiger shark was waving her fins back and forth and wiggling her body from side to side. As Bondar and Jake got closer, they could hear a tiny voice singing:

"The ocean has the sweetest rhythm

It makes you want to swa-a-ay

The ocean has a way to move you

To brighten up your da-a-ay

It makes you move . . . Real smoo-ooth

So sing out and get loose.

—Come on Jazzy, sing with me girl—

Yeah, if you got trouble, if you got pain

Do not get low cause there is no gain

Just listen to the ocean and feel its moves

And soon you'll be grooving like . . . bop, bop, bop, Angelfish dooo."

Bondar and Big Jake were trying to make out who was singing and finally spotted an angelfish swimming along with the tiger shark.

Big Jake said, "Now that's a bit odd."

Bondar was smiling, starting to move to the rhythm of the song when suddenly, out of seemingly nowhere, a huge male tiger shark slammed into the young female.

"Get lost, you loser!" responded the female shark. "I want *nothing* to do with you! Can't you take a *hint?*"

"You *will* be with me or there will be *serious consequences!*" came the large males reply.

Bondar, remembering his past as a fearsome bully, was not going to let this ruffian get away with intimidating the young female. "Hey Jake, get behind him; I'll face him off from the front."

"You got it."

Bondar quickly swept in between the young female and the fierce looking opposer: "It appears this young lady is not interested in you. So, I suggest that you leave this area before you get hurt."

"Get hurt; by who, you? What, are you going to hit me with your hammer? Why don't you butt out and get lost you freak!"

When Big Jake heard the obnoxious shark's stubborn reply, the mammoth humpback responded with a tail slap to the head that knocked the fish about ten feet out of the water. The big male was now unconscious and sinking toward the ocean floor. Bondar looked at Jake and said, "*Sweet*—however, you know what Uncle Gnarls would say?"

"Yeah, yeah, I guess we had better revive him and send him on his way."

The two swam under the lifeless creature, moving it back toward the surface. It did not take long for the fish to come to.

"Now," said Bondar, "let us try this again. If you leave right now and never return, Big Jake and I will let you live. If not, you can join Big Jake and me for a meal, along with a host of our friends. You, of course, will be the meal; *get my drift?* "

Dazed and disoriented, the big shark slowly swam away.

Addressing the angelfish Bondar smiled and said, "I love the song. I was actually, how does it go—starting to move, real smooth?"

The two young ones started giggling. The female tiger shark spoke first; "Thank you so much. We have been trying to lose that bully for weeks."

Bondar replied, "Are you okay? You took a pretty brutal hit."

"Yes, I am okay. He has hit me like that at least a dozen times over the last few days. We figured that by traveling farther north he would finally give up."

Big Jake responded, "I know the type; they never quit until running into overwhelming odds." Flexing his behemoth body he added, "I guess he learned what overwhelming odds feel like."

Bondar looked at the girls and said, "Oh brother, here he goes again; showing off and taking all the credit."

The young ones resumed their giggling.

Bondar continued; "I think some introductions would be in order. My name is Bondar and this is Big Jake."

The young tiger shark blushed; "I am Jazzy and this is Baaya. We have been friends since we were little."

"You have strayed a ways out of your normal habitat, haven't you," replied Jake?

Jazzy answered, "Yes, but we like adventure and have been hearing stories about some fish we really want to meet. Perhaps you have heard of them; Socrates and Poker?"

Baaya added, "Don't forget *Princess Amaya*. She actually has a *kingdom.* I cannot wait to see it. We have heard that it is the most beautiful place in the entire ocean. She and her friends actually fended off a bunch of mean sharks and made them submit to her."

Big Jake looked at Bondar with a goofy grin on his face, realizing that Bondar was one of the sharks little Baaya was referring to.

Baaya continued, "You wouldn't happen to know where to find them, would you? Don't tell me you haven't heard the stories!"

Bondar slumped; "Yes, we have heard plenty of stories. They uh, just happen to be on a little excursion right now. Why don't we arrange a place for you to stay until they return, that is, if you want to hang around for a while?"

Jazzy and Baaya quickly nodded their heads up and down.

Bondar whispered to Jake; "Call the dolphins and have them escort these two to the monoliths; arrange for someone to look after them. I am going to wait here, just in case—well, you know—anything changes."

Chapter 11

Socrates and his friends kept searching out every corner of the plesiosaurs immense domain, frequently observing the humans living in the rock masses above, being very careful because of the humans' proficiency with their spears and their mastery of searching out unwary fish, hitting even the fastest moving target. Yet, they were also predictable. Everything the humans did was on a very precise schedule: regularly going for a swim, harvesting sea plants, driving their captives to work, targeting baitfish schools, you name it; every action being repetitive and programmed to perfection. Socrates was not surprised when, after becoming sufficiently familiar with the bay's surroundings, Two Stars came up with an idea. Addressing NuiMalu she made a suggestion: "You stated that some of your little ones disappeared into small cavities in the far reaches of this cavern and that they are probably too large now to return. Would you mind showing us the location where they disappeared?"

"Not a problem. Though, I would like to know what you are thinking."

"We could try enlarging the openings. Who knows; it is worth a try."

The idea made Nui curious: "and you propose enlarging an opening . . . how?'"

"Well, Kaihula filled me in on the only other creature in the depths of this cavern that any of you trust. She said that he is extremely large and powerful. Maybe he would be up to helping."

Mau, Makana, and Nui looked at Kaihula as if she were crazy.

Kaihula asked, "What, why are you looking at me like that?"

Nui responded, "You told them about . . . *Kabooga?* Are you trying to *scare* them to death?"

Poker, with a hesitant look on his face, asked; "Kabooga, that's a weird name? Is he really big?"

"More like humungus," Nui replied. Then, cocking his head to one side while pretending to pull a baitfish from his teeth, he began speaking out of the corner of his mouth in a comically distorted voice; "Why, he's the biggest *booga* you ever did see."

"Oh, c'mon, stop it," cried Kaihula. She and her parents had broken out into a fit of laughter. Nui just kept up the comical glances, his eyes rolling from side to side. "Other than that, he is . . . sheer terror. Now, do not get me wrong; he is friendly with us. Only, nothing in the world will ever prepare you to meet him. If you don't die from fright when you first see him, he will make sure that you," he hesitated, "how do you say; do bubbles?"

Poker pushed back and asked, "Okay; what is plan B?"

Nui asked Kaihula, "Honey, are you sure about this?"

"Well, have you *ever* come up with a better plan? I really think Two Stars is on to something. You and I can go with them while Mau and Makana stay here with Amaya, Peetie, and the dolphins looking after the newborns. It is worth a try."

"Yeah," continued Nui, "but you know Kabooga is going to try his hardest to scare the daylights out of us."

Glaring at Poker and squinting his eyes, Nui's jaws slowly began curling up exposing his teeth, his animated description of the beast growing in intensity; "He loves to go into his camouflage routine right before his enormous eyes . . . *POP OPEN!* Then, throwing his tentacles out in every direction, he latches onto *anyone* within reach, pulling them slowly toward the darkness of his pulsating throat and into contact with his vicious beak, pretending he is going to—*EAT THEM!* "

Poker quivered in fear, quickly responding once more, "I would at least like to *hear* . . . about a plan B."

Jacko was right behind Poker, nodding in agreement.

Re-addressing Kaihula, Nui continued, "Oh well, I guess we can try enlisting his help. Only, you had better hope his appetite is satisfied just prior to our arrival."

However, NuiMalu suddenly thought of something, his face taking on a quirky smile: "You know, maybe this little expedition will help me get some payback. I have an idea. If we play this out to perfection, I will guarantee that you will share this story with everyone you meet to the end of your days. Oh, this is going to be good."

Uncle Gnarls whispered to Socrates, "I hope you don't mind; Noni and I are going to stay behind with Mau and Makana. We need a break."

KABOOGA

Chapter 12

NuiMalu led the way, descending slowly into the deep reaches of the cavern. Surprisingly, light was remaining consistent the farther they advanced, the beauty of the seascape growing in intensity. Suddenly, old artifacts started appearing, the kinds of objects Socrates had seen fall from fishing vessels. This area did not make any sense. Humans could not live at these depths, so what could explain the presence of these things? Socrates had everyone spread out to examine each item while

NuiMalu and Kaihula discreetly went into hiding. Some of the objects had anemones attached with funny little hair-like follicles dancing back and forth in the current. The delicate motion was so mesmerizing that it put these newcomers in a trance . . . when; Kabooga's roar split the silence like the rumble of a thousand earthquakes. *RAAAAAAAAAH, RAAAAAAAAAAAAAAAH; BOOGA-BOOGA—BOOGA!* Gigantic Tentacles flew out in every direction, wrapping each of Socrates friends in a tight grip, pulling them slowly into the dismal, throbbing, blackness of a throat fronted by an enormous beak. That is when NuiMalu and Kaihula snuck up behind the gigantic octopus, whacked it with their paddle-like limbs, and yelled—*BOOGIE, BOOGIE!* The monstrous cephalopod's tentacles rolled out straight, a huge explosion of effervescent bubbles blowing out from under the alarmed creature, causing it to scream as if being swallowed by a live, fiery volcano. NuiMalu and Kaihula's' laughter instantly rippled through the cavern. "AHHHH-HA-HA-HA-HA; we finally *got* you! Now that was *funny.*" They started chiding; *"We got Kabooga, we got Kabooga."*

*"DANG IT NUI, w*hat do you think you are doing! Oh, you and Kaihula are so *funny;* remind me to *laugh* next time!" Then, unexpectedly, the giant octopus' face got bright pink from obvious embarrassment. Laughingly he added; "Well,

it took a long, long time, but you finally got me. I cannot believe this; I had a perfect record. You had better not tell anyone about this or"—suddenly he noticed how many sets of eyes were focusing on him; grinning an evil grin, he looked around and added, "I sure am hungry; hmm, I wonder who will I have for dinner?"

Nui responded; "Oh, give it up Kabooga! After scaring the bubbles out of us our whole lives, you deserve this!"

"Yeah, I know; but not necessarily in front of a whole group. What are you doing here anyway? Is this all you came for?"

"I would never do that to you. We came because we need your help. Let me explain."

KEAPUALANI

KA'E'A'E'A

KAIMANA

Chapter 13

Nui filled Kabooga in on everything that had happened since Kaihula's arrival with her newborns. Kabooga was immensely impressed with the story of bringing down the pterodactyl and of how Socrates, Poker, and Jacko aided Nui in the battle at the risk of their own lives. Kabooga looked over at Shredder and said, "You must be someone special to merit a rescue like that."

Shredder slumped, being ill at ease with this conversation. His reply; "All I know is that I am getting tired of being squeezed half to death! Doesn't anyone get any *rest* around here?"

Chuckling, Kabooga motioned Nui and Kaihula over to a private place in his garden. "Look, you two, I know the exact area where your young ones disappeared. What is interesting is that, recently, a major surge of energy rocked these depths, something that has not happened for a long time. When it subsided, I went searching this entire area to see if anything had changed. That is when I heard screaming voices coming from an area I could not quite maneuver through. The voices sounded amazingly similar to . . . yours."

Kaihula's eyes teared up; "Kabooga, you don't think . . . ?"

"I am not suggesting anything. I just feel that it would be a good place to begin our search. Get your friends together and follow me."

The jet propulsion of the giant Octopus was incredible. With one blast, he even left Serine behind, and no other fish could match her speed. Kabooga kept on having to wait for the group to catch up while following a serpentine path through a large corridor lined with mineral columns. Due to the sheer quantity of columns, the passageway narrowed to a point that made any further progress impossible for Kabooga, NuiMalu, and Kaihula. It was time to employ Two Stars plan. "Okay," she started, "this is how we will proceed: Our group will start searching out every inch of this corridor for an opening large enough for one of Kaihula's babies to have navigated through. When one is located, we will concentrate only on that one site. Meanwhile, Kabooga can start tearing down these mineral columns to make a wider path through here. We can only hope that the columns are soft enough to break off. That is all we can do for now, so let's get busy."

Kabooga led the charge. Flexing one of his giant tentacles in a show of force, he wrapped it around the first column, ferociously ripping it from the floor of the cavern. Smiling, he then lowered his head as if going into battle and started tearing down every column in site while Nui and Kaihula pushed them off to the side. Kabooga's spirit was contagious, causing the rest of the group to spring into action, checking out every detail of the passageway's structure. It did not take long before Zippee yelled out; "Over here, quick, I have found something."

Located in the cavern's wall, behind one of the huge columns, was a small area of smooth melted stone with a stream of fresh water flowing through. It was immediately obvious that Zippee and Socrates were the only ones small enough to navigate the flow. Socrates turned toward Two Stars and said, "Have the troops ready in case we are chased. Meanwhile, keep Kabooga on the move. If he can make it this far, have him try to increase the size of this opening. Also, have Kaihula shout out her offspring's names. Who knows, they might be in the area. Okay Zippee, let's go."

Swimming through the ultra clear water reminded Socrates of the time he and Amaya raised their heads above the ocean's surface during a storm and feeling the soothing freshness of rainwater on their faces. This water was incredibly pure and he immediately felt its energizing effect. Once clear of the narrow passage, he and Zippee entered the most dazzling region either of them had ever seen. Even Amaya's kingdom could not compare to this. Beautiful plants were lining underwater ledges providing an intriguing dwelling for a variety of colorful sea creatures. Continuing into the shallows, enormous trees became visible above the waterline. Animals of various species were mingling together and feeding on plants growing alongside the banks. There were even smaller animals swinging through the trees and beautifully colored birds flitting from branch to branch. Not one single creature appeared in any danger. This was a place of indescribable tranquility. "I cannot believe this," stated Zippee; "How can a place like this exist in a dimension of complete terror?"

"I have no answer to that," stated Socrates. "However, if Nui and Kaihula's young ones have ended up here, their parents have had no reason for the stress they have endured over the years. It is just too bad that the whole family could not have escaped here ages ago."

Suddenly, a voice cried out in the distance, "Ka`e`a`e`a, Kaimana, Keapualani!" It sounded like Kaihula. She must have reached the opening. Almost instantly, a huge wake built up on the water's surface and three plesiosaurs launched out of water, then tucked their heads, diving straight down. Socrates and Zippee followed.

The very thought of experiencing a family reuniting, was bringing Socrates and Zippee to tears. Yet, one problem remained. The passage was still not big enough for any of the plesiosaurs to navigate through. All they could do was to shout back and forth: "Mom, dad, we are right here! Please, come to us!"

Similarly, Kaihula and NuiMalu were shouting, "Don't worry, we are here to save you!"

The three young ones were thinking, "Save us from what?" However, they kept calling out, overjoyed to hear their parent's voices.

Kabooga finally reached the opening, and sticking one of his tentacles through, gave a mighty tug. Unfortunately, nothing moved, a sharp edge on the backside of the stone mass severely cutting into his tentacle. *"Owww,"* he shrieked, *"Not one of my tentacles!"*

Two Stars felt terrible. Remembering how Bondar and the hammerheads rammed the columns supporting the diamond crystal in the canyon, she scanned the area adjacent to the opening, spotted a slight depression, and slammed her body into the cavern's wall.

Poker yelled out, *"Two Stars,* what are you trying to do, *knock yourself out?"*

She said nothing, automatically circling around and ramming it again. Nui and Kaihula saw what she was trying to do and joined in. After a few more body bashing thrusts, the wall of crusted mineral started buckling and finally gave way. A massive flood of fresh water came gushing into the cavern with Kaihula's brood riding its wake, immediately swarming their parents. Kabooga winked at Kaihula, giving the relieved mother a compassionate smile. He then turned to Socrates and said, "I guess I'll have to get by with only seven tentacles for a while."

Poker swam over to Kabooga and said, "Hey, I once knew an Octopus with seven tentacles named Skully."

Kabooga replied, "Oh yeah, what was the name of his other one?"

"His other one . . . what," came back Poker?

"His other tentacle, what did he call *it?*"

Poker looked confused: "What do you mean, what did he call it?"

"His other tentacle, what did he call it?"

"He had *seven!*"

"Yeah, Skully, right?"

"That's right."

"So, what about his other one?"

"His other one, *WHAT?*"

"Ah, he called it . . . What."

"What?"

"His other tentacle . . . You know . . . What."

"He had seven!"

"Yeah, I get it; Skully and What."

"What are you talking about?"

"That's right, *What* is who I am talking about. Wow, we are finally getting somewhere."

Kabooga thought for a moment, looked around at the group listening in and asking, "Why would he name his tentacles anyway? That makes no sense."

This ridiculous dialogue had everyone in hysterics while watching Poker and Kabooga facing off, staring each other down, and trying to figure out what the other was trying to say. It took a few moments, but Kabooga finally caught on to Poker's meaning of his original statement and broke out into a fit of laughter, his tentacles flailing wildly in every direction and stirring up so much sediment that Ka'e'a'e'a hustled everyone away, retreating to his home through the enlarged passage. Choking from laughter, Nui called back to Kabooga, "We will catch up with you later; in your garden."

Poker, still confused, swam away with Socrates. Glancing back at Kabooga he quipped; "That guy is a half-shell short of a *clam.*"

Chapter 14

Ka`e`a`e`a led the group to a large open expanse of deep-water ledges that were lined with an incredible variety of aquatic plants. What an amazing place for their family to re-unite.

"Mom, dad, we have missed you so much," cried Kaimana; "When we found this place, we were so overwhelmed by everything here, that we just had to explore every detail. We finally decided to return to find you but we could not squeeze back through the opening in the wall. That is when we realized we were trapped."

"I cried for a long time and kept shouting through the opening," added Keapualani; no one ever answered. At first, we were so afraid. We swam around for the longest time just knowing that at any moment something was going to come out and try to chase us down and eat us. Nothing ever did.

We finally loosened up and really began to enjoy being here. You are going to love this place."

Ka`e`a`e`a added; "Trying to calm these two down was tough at first. All Kaimana wanted to do was play while Keapualani kept hiding. We sometimes had to get help from almost every creature here to find her. She was scared because of the crocs chasing us when we were little. Once she finally calmed down, she started forming some good friendships." Turning to his sister he said; "Kea, go find Kooks and Java. Let's introduce them to our family."

Keapualani sped off, as excited as she had ever been.

NuiMalu approached Ka`e`a`e`a, and said; "Son, you are what your name suggests, you are a hero. You have succeeded at keeping your siblings together. Your mother and I are so proud of you."

Ka`e`a`e`a teared up; "This is definitely the best moment of my life." Then, shaking off the emotion, he asked, "Is anyone hungry?"

Poker lit up; "Are there bait schools here?"

"Well, yes, but let me and Kaimana treat you to a special delicacy. You are going to love it. Follow us."

The two ruddy plesiosaurs gave each other a wink and led the group to a miles wide expanse where the water became brackish.

"Over here," called out Kaimana, "Try this."

Poker hurried over, his stomach aching from hunger; "What is it?"

"Here, try some."

Poker looked as if he were going to throw up; "Ewww, what is that? You don't eat that stuff, do you?"

"Mmmmm, yeah, as often as we can," Kaimana replied.

"Oh c'mon," came back Poker, "that is no more than a bunch of slithery weeds; I do not eat weeds!"

"Look closer," said Ka`e`a`e`a, "the stems are lined with shrimp. I will guarantee that this food is one of the best you will ever eat. Go ahead, try it."

Poker edged forward, his friends curiously lining up behind him, watching, and waiting, not one of them volunteering to take the first bite. Poker started bill-whacking the kelp, hoping to dislodge the little crustaceans. Yet, they clung fast. Frustrated at his inability to shake them loose, Poker then opened his mouth, closed his eyes, and bit down. His eyes suddenly popped back open, the grin on his face resembling the look of delight from eating the lobsters at Aunt Dorothy's place months earlier. He shouted, "Oh, yeah, now that is what I'm talkin' about!" He started chomping on the plants like a fish gone mad, his friends quickly joining him in the feast.

After gorging themselves on an endless supply of shrimp laden plants Kaimana grinned and said, "The only drawback to the delicious plants is . . . the, uh, bubbles."

"What bubbles," came back Poker?

Instantly Poker's face took on a troubled look, his stomach rumbling, his back starting to hunch over, and sure enough . . . BLOO-BLOO-BLOO-BLOO-BLOOOOP.

Socrates flinched: *"Sheesh."*

Poker cringed from embarrassment while the others began backing away. Yet, his disconcerted look quickly faded when . . . everyone's stomach started rumbling. Not one of them could contain the gas caused by the plants rapid effect on their digestive tracts. All they could do was yield to the surging pressure and . . . let it go. Kaimana, laughing his head off, shouted; "Hey, let's have a contest."

NuiMalu took him aside and said, "Son, we need to have a little talk."

When the effect of the food finally wore off, Two Stars, Zippee, and Serine were as embarrassed as females could possibly be. Socrates kindly approached them, apologizing: "I am so sorry, that was embarrassing for all of us. That Kaimana is quite the jokester. We will be more cautious the next time he leads us to food. However, I must say, you girls can *splode* with the best of 'em."

The girls' eyes opened wide, being completely shocked that Socrates would say such a thing. They looked briefly at each other, then with furled brows and grins of playful revenge on their faces, turned to Socrates, and grumbled; "Oh, you are going to get it."

Socrates streaked away laughing, and the chase was on.

KOOKS

Chapter 15

The playful scamper ended in an abrupt stop. Keapualani showed up with her two friends, Kooks and Java. Socrates, Two Stars, Zippee, and Serine stared at the three in utter amazement. Keapualani wondered why the newcomers were glaring at her friends . . . causing her to feel unusually uncomfortable.

After a quiet moment, Socrates apologized: "Oh, we are so sorry; it is just that you," directing his attention to Kooks, "look like someone we know."

Just then, Poker showed up with Shredder and Jacko. Poker's impetuous nature immediately took over: "Auntie

Noni, when did you get here? You look great. The water here is making you look younger already."

Kooks looked as if she were going to faint. She politely asked, "Did you say, Noni, Auntie Noni?"

Looking around, Poker shrugged, "Am I missing something? You are Noni, right?"

Kooks and Java huddled together, wondering who these visitors really are and how they know Auntie Noni.

Socrates broke into the conversation; "Uh, Poker, this isn't Noni. This is . . . oh I'm sorry, what is your name?"

The beautiful spotted moray replied, "My name is Kooks . . . and this is my friend Java."

"Well, sharpen my sword," came back Poker, "You sure look a lot like Noni."

Kooks was puzzled and asked, "How do you know my Auntie?"

"How do we know her? Why she's . . ."

Two Stars quickly interrupted, "Poker, why don't you have Ka`e`a`e`a and Kaimana show you guys around while we girls take some time to get acquainted."

"Yeah, okay; But you do see the resemblance, don't you?"

Poker, Jacko, and Shredder sped off with their new friends while Socrates and the girls, along with Kaihula and NuiMalu, remained behind. The first few moments were awkward. Two Stars finally broke the silence by asking, "Have you been here long?"

Java, an elegant chocolate colored dolphin, answered first, "It seems like we have been here for ages. We were exploring a cavern when suddenly; a great quaking started occurring and blinding light engulfed us. The ocean actually caught on fire. A weird, wavy opening appeared in the caverns wall and we escaped through it, ending up here. After taking some time to explore the bay, we tried returning; only, the passage mysteriously . . . disappeared."

Kaihula now entered the conversation with her eyes on Java; "My mate and I cannot remember either of you, and you would have had to enter the secret passage that leads to our bay in order to arrive here. With the distance so far, how could you hold your breath for so long, being a dolphin?"

Java looked over at Kooks who was also trying to figure out what these newcomers were asking. Turning back to Kaihula she answered; "We don't understand. The passage *we* came through is just over there, at the entrance to this bay."

Socrates and his friends appeared befuddled. Kooks and Java looked at each other and shrugged, not comprehending what was wrong. Kooks offered a friendly invitation; "Would you like for us to take you there?"

"Please do," answered Kaihula, "We are obviously confused about all of this."

Lining up behind Kooks and Java for the short trek to the passage, curiosities were running wild. Along the way Keapualani whispered to her mom, "What is going on; everybody is acting so weird?"

Her mom replied, "Mysteries do have that effect."

Kooks and Java led the group to an unusual rock formation at the head of the bay. The rock mass jutted up hundreds of feet above the water line. Some twenty feet beneath the rock mass was a large tunnel that tapered upward. Socrates and his friends followed their escorts through, re-emerging to the water's surface in only seconds. They entered a massive domed cavern with magnificent white mineral columns shooting up from the floor of the cavern. Above the waterline, brightly hued green stalactites were hanging from its ceiling. Kooks then led them through a short passage that ended abruptly in an obscure mass of dark stone.

"This is where we came through," said Kooks. "The stone originally had a strange, wavy form; it seemed our only means of escape from the fire, so we charged through, not knowing where we would end up. We were frightened out of our wits, swimming around disoriented, looking for places to hide, not knowing what to expect. That is, until we met Keapualani. She and her brothers calmed us down and helped us acclimate to this place. We have never had truer friends. Now please, tell us, what do you know about Auntie Noni?"

Two Stars realized that this would be a good time to return to NuiMalu and Kaihula's home. She offered; "Kooks, why don't you accompany us. I think you will be interested in something we have to show you. Serine and Zippee would love to stay here and have Java show them your home. What do you say?"

Kooks hesitated for a moment; yet, she was anxious to find out what Two Stars had in mind to show her. She glanced over at her friend and asked, "Java, are you okay with this?"

Java looked over at Serine and Zippee, smiled, and said, "Yeah, I'll show them the secret overlook. Maybe they can help us figure out what is going on with those strange creatures living on the high ledges."

Chapter 16

Socrates and Two Stars decided it would be best for only Kooks, NuiMalu, Kaihula, and Keapualani to accompany them back to the plesiosaurs domain. His only concern now was to get past Kabooga without scaring Kooks and Kea to death. He had an idea.

Two Stars led the way, gracefully singing a little song. Kabooga was waiting, having everything set to spring another trap. He saw NuiMalu and Kaihula meandering along, chatting and laughing as though they had not a care in the world. Socrates and Two Stars were pretending to check out the Octopus' garden with all its carefully placed relics. Kabooga readied himself to lunge out of hiding when . . . Kooks and Keapualani swam up behind him and in unison said, *"HEY,* are you going to try to scare those guys?"

Kabooga's tentacles flew straight up out of the sand, his wounded tentacle slamming in to a rock. He spun around and screamed, *"OWWWW! WHAAAAT? WHO ARE YOU? WHAT ARE YOU TRYING TO DO?"*

NuiMalu, Kaihula, Socrates, and Two Stars broke into a fit of laughter. Kabooga angrily bristled up, facing off with Nui, and threatening, *"Twice is over the limit pal!"*

Nui, still laughing, replied, "We couldn't let you scare the life out of our daughter and her friend now, could we? You, of all creatures should know; an octopus cannot conceal itself from a moray and a plesiosaur in stealth mode. C'mon, chill out and let me introduce you."

Kooks and Kea shyly swam forward, Kooks apologizing: "We're sorry; we were not trying to scare you." Noticing his wounded tentacle she asked, "Are you okay?"

"Yeah, yeah, I'm okay. I would be better off though if others weren't constantly sneaking up *behind me!*" Once again, Kabooga turned to Nui and said, "This has to *stop!*"

"Oh, so you want to call a truce?"

"Well, at least long enough for my tentacle to heal."

"Only under one condition; you have to be willing to help us if we need you. Until then, we will call out when we pass through so that you will know who is approaching. Any other creature that passes by is still fair game, how's that?"

Kabooga reluctantly nodded; "Fair enough. By the way, where are you going and what happened to the rest of your friends?"

Nui answered, "We are on the way back to our place. We left the others behind and will round them up when we return. Hey, come to think of it, I have a couple of young ones that we can gang up on later. Between you and me, I will bet we can set a new bubble record. What do you say, do we have a deal?"

Kabooga got a huge grin on his face: "I will start getting things ready."

Nui motioned to the others and they continued on their way.

Mau and Makana were in a safe area trying to school Kaihula's newborns while Amaya, Uncle Gnarls, and Auntie Noni watched. Mau was helping the young ones in escape strategy. As large as Mau was, he could move like lightening. The little ones could in no way keep up with him, although they loved playing with Mau and listened to his every word. Mau saw NuiMalu and Kaihula approaching: "Hey you two, how did it go? Did you discover anything new?" Makana also swam over, excited and full of questions. She never managed to speak before Keapualani swam up next to her mother's side. Makana shrieked, "Oh my goodness; *is this . . . ?*"

Kaihula, with tears in her eyes said, "Yes mom, *it's our Kea.* We found her and her brothers; Kabooga helped us locate them. Oh mom, the area is so safe and beautiful: Quick, round up our little ones, there is no reason to stay here any longer."

At that same moment, Amaya raced over to Socrates and greeted him with a big kiss. "You know I never stop worrying about you. You have got to fill us in on what happened."

Uncle Gnarls and Auntie Noni joined in the excitement; "Well Nephew," Gnarls began, "you never cease to amaze me."

"Yeah," came back Socrates, "well, we have a special surprise for you and Auntie." He motioned, and Kooks swam out into the open. Gnarls froze while Noni shrieked . . ."*KOOKS!*"

An overwhelming emotion swept over Kooks, causing tears to well up in her eyes, responding; "*AUNTIE,* how did you get here?"

Neither Gnarls nor Noni could manage a verbal response, they quickly wrapping their bodies around Kooks and hugging her tight.

Socrates, Amaya, and Two Stars gradually backed away to leave the three alone so they could catch up on their lives after years of separation. Uncle Gnarls, with his voice trembling asked; "Socrates—would you, Amaya, and Two Stars stay with us? Whatever Kooks has to share, you probably need to hear."

Socrates replied, "We will stay close Uncle; Take your time."

Chapter 17

Kooks sobbed uncontrollably for several long minutes, trying to determine how she would break the news to Gnarls and Noni about their son, Bohunk. She finally took a deep breath and relaxed: "I know how painful it was for you two when Bohunk tried to take control of the reef after you had spent years working hard, helping all the creatures living there to appreciate the delicate balance of our environment. Everything was going so smoothly. Please forgive me when I say; your son was not you. After all the years of his doing so well, being loved by everyone because of his infectious personality and sense of humor, all of our family noticed a big change in him. He started treating all of us with such disrespect, referring to everyone as freaks, tweaks, and morons. The change grew more pronounced when he fell in with that evil shark, Monegore."

Uncle Gnarls' jaws flared wide at the mention of the name, Monegore. Noni nestled in beside her mate, trying to calm him. Listening intently to the conversation, Socrates, Amaya, and Two Stars decided to move in closer.

Kooks continued: "I tried on several occasions to reason with Bohunk that it would be better for him to wait a while before trying to take your place, giving him time to gain more experience. His defiance to any suggestions made it obvious that Monegore had some sort of mental control over him. Once it became clear that Bohunk was turning everyone against you and was now declaring himself 'keeper of the reef', Monegore, as his so-called 'co-keeper', then proceeded to do what he has done so many times in the past; he led your son into the lair of the Macho Blancos, you know, that nasty band of great whites."

Uncle Gnarls, his countenance bent in fury, broke into the conversation: "If I ever get back to the other side I will find that jerk Monegore and *rip him to shreds!*" Turning to Socrates, Amaya, and Two Stars, Gnarls added; "He was always roaming around like he owned the reef, hanging out occasionally with a band of migrating great whites when all he is . . . is a cross between an anemic nurse shark and a guppy-eyed ratfish. The only reason the Macho Blancos tolerate his presence is his wicked ability to lead naïve young fish into the sharks lair for an easy meal. In return, they let him go on with his petty pretention that he is someone special, someone the reef needs to survive. If only young ones would realize that a desire for prominence and feeling entitled to what someone else has achieved, is what draws predators like Monegore. In the end, their hapless prey loses everything. Only by keeping those impulsive desires in check, do you take away the deceivers advantage. Someday, I will take care of that—*despicable fake!*"

Amaya had never seen Uncle Gnarls so angry.

"There is no need Uncle, that little detail has been handled," replied Kooks.

Uncle Gnarls took a long, deep breath, his eyes still blazing with anger from his short tirade. After taking a moment to calm down he asked, "What do you mean?"

"One day I happened to see Monegore give a wink to one of the great whites. They looked around to check if anyone was watching while encouraging Bohunk to join them in a secret meeting. I decided to follow and cringed when I realized that they were leading him into the secret lair of the Macho Blancos. Bohunk asked, "Hey, why are we *here?*"

Monegore laughed and said, "You punk, your reign is over; I will be taking over now." The sharks quickly circled Bohunk and then began attacking him from every direction. Bohunk fought hard, slashing his head back and forth and maneuvering through the rocks, the way you taught him. Monegore just watched, laughing, waiting for the fight to be over. That is when I could not take it anymore. I lunged out from my hiding place, sinking my teeth into the back of his head, tearing a huge gash in it. Blood started flowing from his wound, triggering an erratic response from his evil cronies. The sharks quickly circled Monegore and viciously tore him apart. They did not even eat him. Even they could see him for what he was: a deceptive, manipulating fraud. They chided the pieces of his sinking carcass boasting, "we do not eat . . . *slime,* you would-be . . . *keeper of the reef.* Like we were going to let that happen, you *loser!*" The Blancos never saw me, I remaining coiled in my hiding place until they left.'"

Holding on to her mate and convulsing from despair, Noni asked, "And . . . what about . . . our son?"

Kooks slumped in sadness; "Oh Auntie, there was nothing left. He was just—gone."

Socrates, Amaya, and Two Stars were heartbroken at hearing this story. They now understood the reason for Auntie Noni's seclusion over the years; it was because of the breakdown of her and Gnarls' relationship with and the subsequent disappearance of their son. Yet Socrates' face took on a curious look, and motioning Uncle Gnarls away from the others he proposed; "Uncle, Kooks said that after the sharks attacked your son . . . there was nothing left. You know how great whites are, they are tacky eaters. Does it make sense that there would be nothing left . . . no blood in the water, no remains, no—*nothing?*"

Gnarls eyes narrowed: "Hmm, yes, it does make one wonder."

Ms. Joleen Teal

Chapter 18

Buddy Gold covertly arranged for a meeting with a wealthy financier whom he was sure would be interested in helping resolve the mystery surrounding recent events in the Bermuda Triangle. Captain O'Brien also entreated FBI agent James Powell to join them in their initial meeting. The Captain's reasoning was that he needed an independent resource who understood the complex management of confidentiality. If any information were to leak out, James could quickly identify the source.

Strolling around the deck, the Captain was breathing in the early morning air while enjoying a cup of rich, aromatic coffee when a cream-colored Bentley, detailed in gold, pulled into the parking lot adjacent to the ship. The driver got out and opened the left passenger door. Buddy stepped out, looked up at Sam standing against the rail on the starboard side of the ship, and winked. Sam raised a brow and thought, "Wow, Buddy was not kidding about the wealthy benefactor." The driver then assisted his primary passenger out of the opposite side of the car. A slender hand clad in a violet silk glove accepted the assistance of the driver and out stepped an extraordinarily beautiful woman. Sam wondered, "Why would Buddy bring a date?" Buddy, dressed in a suit and acting very debonair, held out his arm for the woman's extended hand, and began escorting her aboard the ship.

At the top of the gangplank Buddy smiled, "Sam, I would like to introduce you to Ms. Joleen Teal. Ms. Teal, this is Captain Sam O'Brien."

Sam gracefully bowed his head while keeping eye contact with the new arrival. Her dark skin and strong facial features easily betrayed her Native American descent. Her eyes were the deepest blue of any he had ever seen, rivaled only by the extreme azure of the glacial crevasses in Alaska. Sam smiled and replied; "Ms. Teal, the pleasure is mine; welcome aboard the Ocean Gem. May I show you around, perhaps arrange for some breakfast?"

Joleen Teal had known some dignified men in her life; however, nothing could have ever prepared her for the heart flutter she felt upon meeting this man.

Smiling back, she responded in a slightly Southern accent; "Actually, a morning stroll around the deck and breakfast would be appreciated. Thank you Captain." Withdrawing her hand from Buddy's arm, she offered it to Sam, who politely complied. Feeling slightly embarrassed, Buddy began sticking his hands in his pockets, shrugged, and said, "Yes, I agree . . . an, um, early stroll sounds good."

Sam had a hard time opening a conversation with this elegant woman. Even though his wife had been deceased for a long time, he was a loyal man, his love for his mate still very much alive in his heart. Ms. Teal finally broke the silence; "Buddy shared with me the story of your loss. These past years must have been hard for you and your daughter. I am so very sorry."

Sam looked across the water as it shimmered in the early morning light, his thoughts racing back to the days before his wife became ill. They enjoyed the outdoors so much; swimming and sailing, hiking in the woods and camping out, as simple and perfect a life as anyone could possibly have. Then to have their time together cut so short after the birth of their daughter, left a void he felt impossible to fill. Sam's head slumped in silence for a moment. Then, raising his eyes and gazing over the peaceful surroundings of the bay, he replied, "It has been hard. However, my daughter and I have been carving out a pretty good life for ourselves. We love the ocean; it is our home. The opportunity of living aboard this ship is the best thing that could have possibly happened for us. The owners are amazingly gracious."

Buddy gave way to a slight cough, but kept silent.

Sam asked, "Shall we proceed? Our cook claims he is treating my staff to something special this morning."

Ms. Teal replied, "That is music to my ears, Captain; thank you."

On the way to the dining quarters, Sam could not help feeling perplexed by Ms. Teal's presence aboard his ship. She was obviously Buddy's financial link for their proposed expedition into the Triangle. However, without any explanation from Buddy thus far, talking about it was unusually . . . awkward. Nevertheless, Ms. Teal's charming nature proved a good start to the day.

CHLOE

Chapter 19

The fluffy, soft crepes served with fresh, hot, huckleberry compote were the most sumptuous flavors and aromas Ms. Teal had experienced in her thirty-five years of life. The Captain's choice of his executive chef, Wolfgang Forrest, impressed her. All present remained quiet while Wolfgang and his staff kept pace with the appetites of the Captain and his guests. When it was obvious that all the diners' palates were satisfied, the Captain raised a glass of champagne and proclaimed, "Our complements to the chef." Wolfgang stepped out of the galley and bowed to the spontaneous applause.

It was now time for the Captain to escort his guests to his quarters: "Ms. Teal, Buddy, would you accompany me please?"

The Captain did not expect Tooney to be waiting for him this early in the morning, the corridor leading to his quarters being currently off-limits. However, Tooney had a way of melting the First Mates heart and, unable to resist the pure spirit of this special young man, Corey Coulson allowed Tooney entry to the Captain's quarters prior to Sam's arrival, knowing his boss would not be upset.

When the Captain entered the room, he saw Tooney staring at the nautical map on the wall. Sam smiled and asked him; "Tooney, would like you to meet Buddy's friend, Ms. Joleen Teal?"

Without even turning around, Tooney responded: "Ms. Joleen Teal, the CEO of Teal enterprises, the owner of the Ocean Gem?"

Sam's jaw hit the floor. He looked at Buddy, then at Ms. Teal, then back at Tooney, grabbed a chair, sat down, and said; "Excuse me, I suddenly feel like a total idiot."

Laughter exploded throughout the room. Ms. Teal, who for the first time in years had tears running from her eyes from the humor of the situation, actually coughed up a piece of huckleberry which stuck to the outside of one of her front teeth. Sam could not hold back from doubling over in hysterics at seeing this exotic woman laughing with a goober in her teeth. She had no idea what set him off. He caught his breath for a moment and offered, "P-please Ms. Teal; feel free to freshen up in our guest's s-s-stateroom."

Joleen could not believe it when she grinned in front of the mirror and saw the big hunk of huckleberry blanketing one of her front teeth, compromising her stately, feminine deportment. Yet, feeling unusually comfortable with Sam O'Brien, she continued laughing at the funniest thing that had happened to her in years.

Joleen re-entered the Captain's quarters and in a coy, country tone of voice asked, "You boys will let me know the next time I have a goober in my teeth, won't you?"

Sam and Buddy were still laughing almost uncontrollably and struggling to regain their composure. Tooney, however, blurted out; *"I will tell you Ms. Teal."*

"Why thank you Tooney, it is good to know that chivalry is not dead." Re-addressing Sam, she continued: "Well Captain, shall we pull ourselves together and take a look at what young Tooney has discovered?"

Tooney raced across the room, retrieving his writing tablet. He then sat down and turned to the first page, which contained the equation the government was currently working on. Analyzing and recognizing the formula, Ms. Teal frowned, completely unimpressed; "Why, this is very interesting young man. It is too bad that all attempts to resolve the flaws in this equation have failed so miserably." She asked Buddy, "Didn't the government mothball this idea about five years ago?"

Buddy re-directed her attention back to Tooney who then flipped the page, displaying his revision. Scanning each line, Ms. Teal's eyes grew wider and wider, her face progressively turning pale, she instantly comprehending the significance of the formula. Kneeling on the floor beside Tooney, her voice quivering, she gently caressed his hand and asked, *"Depth to pressure ratios?"*

Sam smiled and replied, "That was my first question. However, he is not done. Go ahead, show her Tooney."

Tooney turned to the third page, revealing the element's transformation into a liquid gel form. Ms. Teal went numb, her hands shaking, her mind racing: *"How many know of this formula?"*

"Only those in this room," responded Buddy.

Impulsively kissing Tooney on his cheek, she then jumped to her feet; "I am in, be ready to leave in thirty minutes."

Captain O'Brien threw his hands up: "Now hold on; there are others that have to be considered. What's more, we will not be going anywhere without Tooney's parents and his grandmother. So, whatever arrangements have to be made, make them with their approval."

Ms. Teal's demeanor took on a semblance of defensiveness. No one had upstaged a single decision of hers in at least 10 years. Struggling to control her urge to dominate an outcome she could not help giving Sam a stone cold stare; "May I ask who else is so important to our research?"

Just then, Corey Coulson opened the door and said, "Captain, James Powell is here sir; may I show him in?"

Ms. Teal calmed immediately when James strolled in. She asked, "Why James, how have you been? You are not somehow linked up with these three scientific scoundrels, are you?"

"Ah, c'mon Joleen, you know I always scrape the bottom of the barrel."

Sam and Buddy stood silent, wondering how these two knew each other.

Detecting Sam and Buddy's curiosity, James explained: "Joleen and I studied police science together in college. Out of sheer boredom with her classes, she decided to change her major to analytical physics. She landed a PhD in only three years. After graduating, I joined the Agency and she went independent which, from the looks of things, was a good move on her part. So, tell me Sam, what is so important that you have to have my office involved; what is Tooney up to now?"

"I will explain on the way," replied Sam. "I sure hope you have some vacation time coming, because the department cannot in any way know of or be involved in what we are planning. In fact, everything we do from here on out has to remain confidential. Are you absolutely sure, you want to be a part of this? It could cost you your job."

"Knowing you Sam, I would not miss it for the world. Moreover, if I lose my job, I am sure Joleen will find something for me to do. Am I right, cousin?"

Sam gasped, "You are kidding . . . right?"

James and Joleen then proceeded to give each other a big hug and the Captain replied, "No, I guess you are not kidding."

Suddenly the door to the Captain's quarters flew open and a voice rang out; *"Daddy, I'm home!"*

Chloe ran across the room, leaping into her father's outstretched arms. "Oh, sweetheart, I have missed you so much. How was your visit with your cousins?"

"I had the most wonderful time. They took me to probably every theme park in Orlando. Look, look what I got you."

Chloe ran back to the door and asked Corey Coulson to help her with a box. Corey brought the heavy container in and placed it on the table. Sam asked, "Well young lady, what have we here?"

Upon opening the box, a bright glimmer reflected off a large, highly polished, antique ships bell with unique scrolling gracing its lower rim.

"Wow," interrupted Ms. Teal, "a Spanish artifact. A bell like that is amazingly rare."

Chloe looked at Ms. Teal, then at all the others in the room, and then back at her dad. She tugged at her father's shirt and asked in a whisper, "Who are these people?"

Sam smiled and said, "If I can have everyone's attention, I would like to introduce you to my daughter Chloe. Chloe, this is FBI agent James Powell. Standing next to him is the owner of our ship . . . Ms. Joleen Teal, along with my old friend Buddy Gold. Last, but certainly not least . . . I would like to introduce you to Tooney. He is the young man whose actions helped save our ship."

Chloe's eyes beamed upon hearing the name, Tooney. She had been following the news reports about what had happened to the Ocean Gem on the last leg of its cruise to the Bahamas. Young people from all over the country were trying to find out more about Tooney's adventure with the dolphin and here he was; present in a meeting in her dad's quarters. Chloe shyly stood close to her dad while Tooney sat in a chair with a slight grin on his face, obviously embarrassed to meet a girl, especially one that appeared interested in meeting him. Somehow, he seized the courage to look up and say, "I like the bell."

Chloe responded, "Here, check out these cool markings."

Just then, there was another tap on the door. Cracking the door slightly, Corey whispered, "Captain; Charlie and Carlynn are here Sir; may I show them in?"

"Yes, of course, thank you Seaman Coulson."

Tooney's parents walked into the room, and gazing over at their son, were amazed to see him so openly responding to such an outgoing little girl. Chloe did not perceive anything unusual about Tooney . . . other than a little shyness. She carried most of the conversation while Tooney focused intently on the scrolling around the bell's rim.

Chapter 20

Tooney's parents were excited about the Captain's proposal that they go along on a scientific expedition. Charlie had been out of work for three years, having lost his job as an aeronautical engineer. His specialty was developing prototypes for extreme altitude, hypersonic aircraft. The company he worked for wanted to transfer him to Europe, he turning down their proposal. They took his rejection of the job as an act of disloyalty to the company and gave him his walking papers. His wife's current employment was as a high school biology teacher. This time of year did not interrupt her work schedule, being the third week of July, and school not resuming until September. Together, Charlie and Carlynn kept their lives simple and manageable, allowing them the latitude to spend plenty of time with their special son. Tooney's grandmother chose to stay at home and take advantage of an extended vacation with some of her aged friends.

Joleen Teal left the ship early while the Captain helped Tooney and his parents decide what to take along on what could turn out to be a lengthy adventure. Ms. Teal returned in less than an hour with her driver Donavan Clay chauffeuring her in a stretch Hummer limousine with enough room for at least ten guests including their luggage. Observing Joleen's obvious excitement while helping her guests load their gear in the vehicle, Sam stated; "You certainly don't let any grass grow under your feet, do you?"

Ms. Teal replied; "nothing is worse than complacency. Reliving past tragedies got old in Choctaw country where James and I grew up. We felt cramped for room to 'spread our wings' and pursue our goals. Now do not get me wrong; we loved growing up in Oklahoma where our parents raised us in the proud tradition of contributing something positive to the world. Therefore be assured Captain, James and I appreciate our heritage. We, how would you say, carry it with us wherever we go. Our indigenous spirit is what drives our thirst for adventure."

Donovan taxied to the airport in only a matter of minutes. A private jet was waiting and ready for take-off.

The Dassault Falcon 900 needed very little runway and was airborne in seconds. Scanning the cabin, the Captain was curious, wondering what had happened to Ms. Teal. Some forty-five minutes into the flight, he heard her voice over the intercom inviting him to come forward into the cockpit. It did not surprise him when he opened the door and saw Ms. Teal piloting the plane. She opened the conversation: "Please, Captain, take a seat. I could use a good co-pilot and if my information is correct, you have a pilot's license."

Sam replied, "Yeah, but, this is way out of my league."

"Take the co-pilot's seat anyway; I can use some company. By the way, keep an eye out because I think we are getting close to the guesstimated co-ordinates where the Ocean Gem nearly went down."

Looking at the beautiful ocean from this vantage point was a rare treat for the Captain. Yet, it was certainly no substitute for the thrill of actually being on the water. Nevertheless, he kept his eyes peeled over the vast expanse of what he claimed as his home. It took only moments before he saw something unusual: *"What's that,"* Sam called out!

Joleen's eyes quickly locked on to the area Sam was pointing to: "Did you see something?"

"Yes, over there. Something extremely bright just flashed off the ocean. Do you see it? Look portside about eleven o'clock!"

"I can't see anything. Are you sure it wasn't just a refection off the water?"

"Hey, if there is anything I know, it is reflections. That was no ordinary flash of light. Do you see a ship or anything?"

"I do not see a thing."

"Check your co-ordinates. Where are we?"

Ms. Teal's face showed some concern. "Captain, we have a problem. Our navigational equipment is *frozen!*"

"Is the plane in jeopardy?"

"I don't think so. Please, call Tooney in here, *quick!*"

Sam tried to appear unconcerned as he re-entered the cabin and asked Tooney if he would like to view the cockpit. The little boy handed Chloe his writing pad and raced from his seat. Chloe jumped up and followed. As soon as the cockpit door closed behind them Ms. Teal asked; "Tooney, a plane leaves the cape airport at 10:37 a. m., progressively accelerating to 350 knots and an altitude of twenty thousand feet on an East/Southeast heading of 115 degrees. Assuming easterly headwinds are 15 miles per hour, where would we be at 11:29 a.m.? Get your map and show me, *quickly now.*"

Tooney ran into the cabin, then back into the cockpit with his map and pointed; "Right there."

Assuming 90 seconds have passed, what can we do to find the same spot?"

Tooney looked out the cockpit window, spotted the position of the sun, and said, "Bank left 6 degrees and reduce speed to 280 knots."

"Tooney, you do not understand; my instruments are not working."

"Pull throttle back 20 percent. Turn yoke left 1 inch. Hold it there."

Sam O'Brien and Chloe could only look on in silence as Joleen followed Tooney's instructions exactly.

"How much time do we have Tooney," Joleen asked?

"127 seconds," came the reply.

Joleen glanced at Sam and said, "Okay, Captain, keep your eyes peeled; we may not get another chance."

To the second, a flash appeared that was unmistakably something other than the sun's reflection off the ocean.

Looking out the window, Tooney grinned from ear to ear; *"The canyon! Ms. Teal found the canyon!"*

Sam asked, "How can you be sure? Do you see something?"

"Sun reflecting off crystal," answered Tooney.

"What crystal," asked Ms. Teal?

"It is something that Tooney says he saw when he was in the water while our ship was in distress," replied Sam.

Ms. Teal still could not get her instruments to respond so she pointed to Tooney's map and said; "Tooney, my island is that little spot just south of Bermuda. How do we get there from here?"

"Turn yoke slightly right. Count 15 seconds; then, bring it back and increase speed by 20 percent."

Ms. Teal once again followed Tooney's directions and finally, after some tense moments, breathed a sigh of relief, her navigational panel lighting up. *"Oh, Tooney;* I have no idea what I would have done without you. *Thank you.* Now

I know what your Captain must have been up against on your cruise through this area. Sam, would you mind showing Tooney and Chloe back to their seats while I double-check my location with the Bermuda flight tower? We will be landing in about an hour. I assume that is correct, right Tooney?"

"Fifty-seven minutes and twenty-three seconds," came the reply.

When Chloe and Tooney were back in the cabin and safely buckled in their seats, Chloe looked at Tooney and asked, "How did you do that? How did you know the proper degree to turn the plane and . . . how much Ms. Teal needed to adjust her speed and . . . how long it will take to get to where Ms. Teal is taking us? There is nothing out here to mark anything."

Tooney grinned, glancing over at Chloe through the corners of his eyes: "Ms. Teal gave me data and I can see the position of the sun. Its relationship to the earth at any time of day is like a compass."

"Yeah, but . . . you are ten years old. Einstein could not do what you just did."

"I don't know; I see things in my mind. The matrix is pretty simple."

"Can you teach me about the matrix?"

"Okay, hand me my writing pad."

Chloe listened intently to Tooney's explanation of planetary and solar relationships while at the same time drawing a detailed diagram of the solar system. Charlie and Carlynn were astonished at how quickly Tooney was bonding with Chloe, in addition to his special connection with the Captain and Ms. Teal. Charlie reached into his travel bag, pulled out his laptop, and continued documenting his observations of Tooney's social progress. He felt an urge to share his son's experience with the National Autism Foundation, hoping that whatever triggered his son's abnormal introversion reversal could be helpful to other families.

Chapter 21

Exactly on time, Ms. Teal's voice came over the intercom preparing her passengers for landing. The touchdown was as smooth as if the jet had landed on a huge ball of cotton. Sam O'Brien took the lead exiting the plane. Dense tropical plants were cloaking the airstrip on all four sides while the sound of waves crashing against a cliff could be heard reverberating in close proximity to their location. Ms. Teal began escorting her passengers along a path through the dense foliage. The path was well manicured and within' a hundred yards opened up to reveal a wooden suspension bridge spanning a narrow gorge. Below the bridge flowed a beautiful river, its life generating from the cloudy peaks of the three thousand foot high mountain range above. The river traveled only fifty feet past the bridge before cascading four hundred feet into the sea below. Ms. Teal paused, directing her guests to a safe viewing pad overhanging the edge of the cliff. This strategic position revealed one of Earth's truly unique phenomena. The tide was in and every twenty seconds or so the ocean waves would fill a deep cave at the bottom of the cliff, super-charging a narrow channel beneath the falls. Under immense pressure, the water would then explode upward through the waterfall . . . creating for a split second an anomaly where the cascading water fanned out horizontally, suspending it in mid air, each time highlighted by a misty, perfect-circle rainbow. All stood motionless as the powerful waves forced this repetition at least two to three times every minute.

Ms. Teal broke the silence after allowing her guests a sufficient amount of time to absorb the tranquility of this marvel of creation. "I am glad that we were able to arrive at high tide. You are seeing the falls at their zenith. This is the only place on earth where the geological convergence of merging waters creates a gravity defying suspension in mid air. The perfect circle rainbow is like icing on a cake. Please, shall we continue?"

Ms. Teal led the group across the suspension bridge and along a grassy path, arriving at the entrance to a large tunnel carved into the base of one of the islands hillsides. An entourage of scientists was waiting to greet their employer and her guests. Ms. Teal made all the introductions, leading the way into the tunnel and personally narrating the tour; "The first hundred feet of tunnel is lighted with reflective panels that are fed with sunlight from well placed mirrors outside. A solar generator as well as a dozen windmills located on the windward side of the island supplies all the additional energy required to run this facility. You will notice the paver stones you are walking on have grass growing in between them; this helps to regulate the temperature inside the tunnel. We have found that the combination of stone and greenery keeps the tunnel at a steady 68 degrees, which is a welcome break from the constant 80 degrees plus temperature of the island." Well inside the tunnel, Ms. Teal had everyone stop. Pulling a cell phone out of her backpack, she dialed a number. Instantly, an eight-foot square span of the tunnels wall slid to one side revealing an elevator door, which automatically opened when its sensors detected the outside wall rolled out of place.

"Cool," remarked Chloe, "that is way cool. Where does it go?"

"Let's find out," Ms. Teal replied.

Once inside, the large elevator doors closed and their descent began. The well-lighted cab featured panels of solid acacia wood with nautical carvings of sea creatures. Tooney held his mother's hand and smiled while pointing out a carving of a dolphin. The ride ended in about 45 seconds. Sam O'Brien swallowed hard when he and his entire team stepped out of the elevator and onto the deck of a waiting sky-tram. All the guests remained silent, boarding the tram with their curiosities running wild. As the tram pulled away, Ms. Teal continued her narration: "Friends, this is my home." All gasped as an amazing city, built into a natural expanse located in the belly of the island, became visible. "The entire population of this island is from various indigenous tribes of North America. Originally funded by grants from the Choctaw, Cherokee, Sioux, and Navajo nations, our sole purpose is to develop earth friendly technologies for future generations. We have been very successful and have not only repaid the grants that made all of this possible, but have established a permanent and self-sustaining foundation for the education of our tribes. We are committed to forging ahead instead of concerning ourselves with tragedies from the past. Our first stop is right up ahead."

Stepping out of the tram was like walking into a dream. The tram platform merged with numerous stone paths leading to well spaced, colorful lodges. Each lodge housed up to four people, being circular in shape, allowing a communal sitting area in the center for at least twenty. "These are our guest facilities and you are welcome to pick out whichever lodge agrees with you. All seventeen of them have unique décor supplied by Native American vendors. Take some time to walk through them and choose the one that makes you feel most comfortable. You will also notice that at both ends of the main walkway are commissaries with an amazing variety of food choices. Our chefs will instruct you on the menu preparations and you can eat to your heart's content. I will return in a couple of hours and we can continue your orientation."

Ms. Teal then re-boarded the tram, allowing her new arrivals time to acquaint themselves with their surroundings.

Sam looked at James and asked, "Did you know anything about this? She is your cousin, right?"

James' eyes were rolling around in his head like loose marbles: "I had no idea Joleen was up to anything remotely like this. I knew about the original grants, but did not question their target. I never had any reason to ask about it. The two of us sought completely different career paths and, except for a family reunion ten years ago, never communicated after that. I have to admit, she is an amazing woman."

Buddy Gold remained speechless while strolling around and taking in all the magnificence of this incredible place.

Then, all of a sudden, he burst out in laughter: "Look at all of this, just look at it; how resilient can people be? The government thought that by stripping the tribes of their dignity, they were going to just dry up and blow away. Well, *hello*, they obviously guessed *wrong*." He then turned to Tooney and said, "As smart as you are young man, *you* must be native American."

Charlie answered Buddy, "Now that you mention it, both of my parents descended from the Iroquois, and my wife's roots are Seminole. Wow, this is the first time I have ever felt so connected to my heritage." He then pulled Tooney to his side and said, "We have big shoes to fill son."

Chloe, who had been wandering around, appeared from the end of one of the paths and blurted out, "Quick Tooney, come with me; you will not believe what I have found!" She held out her hand for Tooney, expecting him to take hold of it. He paused, looking at her outreached hand and then up at his mom. Carlynn looked her son in his eyes, nodding her approval. Tooney struggled to reach out, but after a brief moment of uncertainty, extended his hand. Chloe's touch sent chills up his spine and a smile of acceptance to his face. The two raced off to check out Chloe's discovery, the rest quickly following to see what it was that had Chloe all worked up. At the extreme east end of one of the paths, a circular stone staircase climbed about one hundred feet to another viewing pad. From this perch, the entire city in all its magnificence was visible. A wide river channel, its banks lined with tropical plants, was snaking its way through the middle of this subterranean metropolis. Strangely, the water of the river gently surged back and forth as if it were—breathing. Once again, all stood motionless, observing the life of the earth in its purist form.

When Ms. Teal returned, she found her guests quietly strolling around, embracing the overwhelming splendor of her enchanting city. "Please everyone; let's re-board the tram. Your tour has just begun."

For the next hour, the tram slowly circled the spectacular complex. Ms. Teal pointed out the housing facilities for the island's residents, manufacturing plants, as well as scientific laboratories for advanced ship design and deep-sea submersible technologies. The tram finally came to a stop in front of a laboratory marked, *New Discoveries*, a group of scientists standing at the ready for Ms. Teal's arrival. While her guests were exiting the tram, Ms. Teal called Tooney forward: "Tooney, would you mind showing these men your writing pad?"

Tooney handed it over without a word.

Ms. Teal continued: "Gentlemen, what you are about to see is going to change history."

Joseph Hawk, the leader of the scientific team, graciously took the pad from Tooney's hands. Looking at the first page, Joseph smiled, recognizing the faulty, decades old formula. However, after turning to the second page, his hands started shaking. Turning to the final page, he froze. After a moment of contemplation, his eyes filling with wonder, he asked Joleen; "How many know of this formula?"

"Only my guests," responded Ms. Teal. "Shall we . . . get to work?"

Chapter 22

Socrates could not stop stressing over the uncertainty of his friend's circumstances. He knew that their safety was of primary importance, yet witnessing the mistreatment of unfortunate humans was equally troubling to his heart. Coupled with pterodactyls from above and the crocs on the other side of the passage to Nui's home, Socrates was at a loss. "Are there any other horrors we need to be aware of," he asked NuiMalu?

"Only the eels," was Nui's reply.

"What eels?"

"Electric eels; only these are much larger and far more vicious than any you have ever seen. They rarely make an appearance though, unless there is a significant disturbance in their vicinity."

"And I suppose this just might be one of those vicinities?"

"Um, yeah," replied Nui, "as a matter of fact, this is one of their playgrounds; especially when a fight ensues."

Socrates smiled . . . the wheels in his head racing with ideas. He turned to Mau and asked, "What would be your best guess as to the numbers of the crocs and the pterodactyls?"

"We know for certain there are only seven crocs in the area where you first arrived. They have never managed to find the secret passage that leads here. In addition, from our last count, I suppose not more than twenty to thirty pterodactyls still exist."

"Is there any way of making sure?"

"Yeah, we can fake a feeding frenzy. That is one thing that gets them *all* stirred up."

"And how do we do that?"

Mau grinned and said, "Move aside and get ready for some action."

Mau, Makana, NuiMalu, and Kaihula swiftly swam into the middle of the bay and dove to the bottom; then in perfect unison streaked to the surface and leaped out of the water, faking a feeding frenzy. After splashing around for a couple of moments, they submerged and jetted off. The activity on the surface was pure mayhem. Small boats were launching from shore, the evil humans abandoning everything in response to the disturbance in the middle of the bay. At the same time, pterodactyls swooshed across the sky while electric eels started swarming the surface.

Chuckling, Mau asked, "Okay, how many is that?"

Socrates and his friends were in no hurry to venture out of the safety of their secret lookout to count anything in the midst of this flurry of madness. Mau, still grinning and detecting their hesitation, added; "No problem, Nui and I will take care of the count."

Mau and Nui quickly sped away to assess the oppositions numbers. Returning some time later Mau reported; "Well, at last we know there are exactly twenty three pterodactyls and about a hundred human bad guys."

"And the eels," asked Uncle Gnarls?

"There is no limit to their number."

"So, what we have here is a D.K. standoff, am I right," asked Socrates?

Nui thought about it for a moment and then asked, "Okay, what is a D.K. standoff?"

Little Peetie and Schooner were within' earshot of the conversation. Peetie nudged Schooner and said under his breath, "Listen, and *learn* from the master."

Socrates cocked his head to one side, cleared his throat, resumed eye contact with Nui, took a deep breath, and stated; "That's when—you think you understand what to do when in reality you are not sure that what you are going to try is really perceived by yourself or anyone else. You just stick to your hypothetical plan and hope for the best."

"Um, yeah," replied Mau, "I couldn't have said it better myself. By the way, what are we going to do?"

Little Peetie and Schooner hovered motionless for a moment, thinking about what Socrates meant by the bazaar phrase. They turned to Amaya who was staring at Socrates as if he were crazy. He smiled at her, and winked. She turned her head aside, pursing her lips while trying to control her urge to laugh, knowing Socrates was only kidding. Peetie and Schooner caught on and started chuckling, Peetie whispering to Schooner, "see what I mean; the guy is a genius." They quietly backed off from the rest of the group, continuing their laughter. However, Socrates did have an idea: "Kaihula, gather your little ones. Kooks, take Kaihula and the newborns along with Noni, Makana, and Keapualani back to your home. When you arrive, send our entire team, along with Ka'e'a'e'a, back here. Two Stars, find Jibber, Stony, and Rocky. They are around here somewhere. I have a plan."

Kooks swam up to Socrates and stated, "Just one thing; one of the captors is not like the others, she regularly taking the captives food, being attracted to one of their number. I think she is in love."

Socrates got a curious look on his face; "You know about the humans?"

"Where we live, there is a lookout in the shallows that must front this same bay from the other side. We have observed these same creatures for years. A huge, tight web blocking the channel entering the bay prevents anyone from escaping."

From Socrates perspective, this information added another essential element to his preparation. His plan was to send Two Stars and Peetie along with Kooks in order to figure out the best way to compromise the web just enough to rescue the captives. Addressing Peetie he explained; "I would like you to help figure out an escape plan. Do you remember how the rockfish used the kelp to close up the fishing net after the hammerheads drew it tight?

"Yeah, that was so awesome."

"Well, see if you can come up with a similar method to open the web for an escape. The separation will have to be undetectable once we rescue the captives though. Do you think you can handle that?"

Peetie responded, "Aww, *dude*, I am gonna make this *happen!*"

Socrates smiled, watching the little rockfish speed away. He then turned to Kooks and continued; "take your time. We have to plan everything with precision. Also, inform Kabooga that we need his help figuring out our strategy."

As Kooks led her group away, Socrates turned to Uncle Gnarls and asked, "Have you observed anything about the humans that might give us an edge in this little escapade?"

"Actually, there is one thing that is really unusual. I think it would be best though if we wait for Poker and the others, so that together we can see what we are going to be up against."

It took awhile rounding up all the participants, but finally those Socrates requested arrived at his location. Uncle Gnarls then led them to an area adjacent to a large bluff. He whispered, "Be patient and keep still; watch what the humans do when they arrive in front of that structure."

On a ledge, close to the shore, stood a large wide column with a coved opening in the front. Inside sat what looked like a small meteorite. No one spoke while awaiting the arrival of the captors. Finally, the evil humans, with scowls on their faces, came marching in, lining up in rows in front of the column, the head of their charismatic leader draped in twists of seaweed. They dropped to their knees and bowed before the column, all the time loudly chanting.

"What is it you think they are saying," asked Amaya?

"I have no idea," replied Socrates, "after all, what can you say to a piece of rock that is all that important?"

All the fish started chuckling. "Is the thing moving," asked Jacko?

"Not currently,' replied Nui.

"What do you mean by that," asked Socrates?

"Well, it did move when they picked it up and placed it there. Ever since then I would have to say, um—uh—no; it has pretty much just laid there."

"What is up with the seaweed draped around that one guy's head," asked Shredder?

"I don't know," came back Poker, "Maybe they are going to feed it to the rock to see if it makes bubbles."

A roar of laughter shattered the silence. "Shhh," urged Gnarls, "keep quiet . . . they cannot detect we're here."

"Look," said Nui, "look at what they are doing now."

When the humans stood up, they filed past the column, each one bending over, and kissing the object inside.

"That is weird," replied Socrates.

Stony nudged Rocky: "Remember when we were little; you know the time we replaced Jibbers favorite piece of coral with an old oyster shell?"

"Oh, ha-ha," replied Jibber, "you two are about as funny as bubbles in a bait ball."

"*Yeah,*" smiled Stony, "and you know how funny that is."

Rocky adding: "I love that, everyone has their mouths open and everything."

At this point, the laughter was uncontrollable.

Socrates' curiosity was peaking over Stony's comment: "So, what are you two suggesting?"

"Wouldn't it be funny if we exchanged that little item with—he thought for a moment—maybe—hmm—a clam?"

Socrates' eyes narrowed, his grin widening; "The response would be interesting, especially if we coupled it with some activity on the surface. Perhaps we could create enough of a diversion for Kooks and Two Stars to help the captives to escape. Kabooga, you could reach that column with one of your tentacles, couldn't you."

Kabooga smiled, "Oh yeah, and that little beauty would look real nice in my garden. Moreover, I know just the kind of clam to replace it with—a *snapper clam*. It has a powerful, thick shell and can live out of water for quite some time. If you touch the shell, it will open for just a moment, revealing a colorful, luminescent inner lining, which makes it hard to resist reaching in and stroking the beautiful surface. However, once the interior is touched, the shell will suddenly slam shut and you will regret ever having laid eyes on it. Hey Poker, maybe your friend Skully had the same thing happen to him; perhaps . . . 'What' . . . was actually . . . 'Smashy'."

Poker was not amused. He whispered to Socrates, "I'm telling you, he is a half shell short. Somewhere in that doofer's past, someone bit him between his eyes."

Kabooga comically continued; "If one of those maniacs tries to kiss the clam while its shell is gaped open—whoa, can you imagine; can you say—permanent damage? If they can ever peel it off his mouth, his lips are going to look like a bulging cross-section of brain coral for the rest of his life."

Taking in the reaction of his friends to Stony's suggestion, Socrates urged; "I say . . . let's go for it."

Nui agreed; "Yeah, it's time we put this madness to an end."

With that, all lined up behind Nui, silently retreating to put together their plan of action.

Chapter 23

Back on Ms. Teal's private island, Buddy Gold was working feverishly with James Powell cataloguing the events of the Ocean Gem on the day of its narrow escape in the Bermuda Triangle. Captain O'Brien and Corey Coulson filled them in on their crew's reaction while Buddy and James read the Captain's log. Suddenly, Buddy jumped up from the table in a panic, and running over to a nautical map on the wall, blurted out, "That's it, that's got to be part of the answer!"

"What are you talking about," asked James?

"Look at the date of the 'event'; June 28th."

"So, what is your point?"

"My point is that on June 25th an enormous coronal mass ejection occurred . . . you know, a solar flare off the sun, and earth was in its path. Our planet's survival was actually in jeopardy. Incredibly, our atmosphere deflected its intensity. It was traveling at a speed of one million miles per hour through space, which took just under four days to reach us. The position of the sun on June 28 was at its highest peak over the Ocean Gem's guesstimated co-ordinates in the Triangle on that very day. That could well explain what triggered the fiery phenomenon that put your ship in jeopardy. Let's think now, what do we know about the Bermuda Triangle?" Buddy started pacing back and forth across the room, his head hanging in silence and serious contemplation: "Okay, in 1492 Columbus saw strange atmospheric lights that he could not explain in the same area your ship got into trouble. In addition, in December 1945, Flight 19 composed of five FT28 torpedo bombers went on a training mission into some of the very same flight space we traveled through getting to this island. After only four hours, they disappeared into seemingly . . . thin air. The PBM patrol plane sent out to find them also disappeared. Prior to that, in 1918, the U.S.S. Cyclops, a ship employed by the Naval Overseas Transportation Service disappeared after a brief stop in Barbados. All 500 crewmembers were lost. What all of these tragedies have in common is . . . the one and a half million square miles of ocean that we currently refer to as the Bermuda Triangle. What is even more interesting though, is that about six decades ago, after the loss of Flight 19, the

National Geophysical Data Center picked up a 'bloop' on its data recorder; it is a characteristic sound made by an early type of radio receiver. The sound is detectable up to three thousand miles away and the source . . . was never established."

"Your point being," Sam queried.

"Well, it adds one more link to our mystery; maybe, just maybe, someone out there actually survived. Let's call Tooney in here and see what we can find out about the canyon and the crystal he claims he saw."

Sam quickly located Tooney and Chloe who were sitting at a desk in an adjacent office with Charlie and Carlynn. Tooney had them engaged in a simple explanation of his theory of planetary matrix dynamics. Sam kindly interrupted, "Charlie, Carlynn, would you mind bringing the kids into the Geo-Mapping office? We have some questions for Tooney."

Charlie raised his hand slightly and whispered, "Give us a couple of minutes Captain; Tooney is just wrapping up our lesson."

Tooney resumed his drawing and his simple explanations. Watching Tooney's parents sit there like students in a classroom, with their 10-year-old son teaching them about the structure of the solar system, was as amazing a thing as the Captain had ever witnessed. Sam quietly stood in the doorway, patiently waiting for Tooney to wrap it up.

Buddy arranged the chairs in the Geo-Mapping office in a semi circle. There was no reason to leave anyone out of the conversation. Chloe took her seat next to Tooney while his parents sat on his other side. "Okay," started Buddy, "Tooney, you pointed out on the map where you saw the canyon and the crystal. Did you see them well enough to illustrate them?"

Tooney did not say a word. He simply got out of his chair, walked over to a green-board hanging on the office wall, and started drawing. His first image resembled a volcano with an extended cone. The top of the cone was flat with a large round opening. The three dimensional image revealed the mount being hollow on the inside and widening out toward the bottom. In the center, at the floor of the interior, Tooney drew a large circle and proceeded to connect hexagonal lines across the surface. This three dimensional image did indeed appear to be a crystal with an incredible amount of facets. Once finished, Tooney started drawing straight lines out of the image in every conceivable direction. He then put down his chalk and took his seat. The drawing was of amazing clarity and for a few moments, no one said a word. Buddy finally broke the silence; "Thank you Tooney. By the way, did you see anything else in the canyon?"

"Only . . . what was stuck to the sides."

"What was stuck to the sides?"

Tooney slumped and in a sad tone responded, "Old ships and planes."

All in the room stared at Tooney's drawing on the green-board for several minutes, the air in the room growing thick with mystery. After a few quiet moments, Chloe turned to Tooney and asked, "Where did the dolphin take you?"

Tooney went back to the board and resumed his sketch. He began by drawing a line from the top of the mount to a nearby cavern. He then proceeded with details of the cavern, including the spiraled opening leading to the large open-air expanse where the dolphin deposited him. He then drew a diagram of large half-man/half-fish images along with what he previously described as the 'wavy-window'. Tooney then drew a picture of himself, depicting his extending his arm into it and saying, "Tooney's hand did not get wet."

Sam O'Brien's mind was once again racing, the pieces of the story captivating him. He asked, "Are all of you thinking what I am thinking?"

Surprisingly Chloe chimed in; "Are we talking about the lost city of Atlantis?"

Sam got a smile on his face, stared at the floor for a moment, then looked up at his daughter; "You are . . . familiar with Atlantis, are you?"

She responded, "Well the guy who sold me the ships bell told me a few stories. I believe he was trying to make me think the bell had something to do with a search for the city. I just thought it was cool and bought it for you."

James Powell was stroking his chin, absorbing the conversation. He suddenly stood up and spoke; "We need to share this information with Joleen and her team of advisors. I think we are in over our heads."

Buddy looked at James and responded; "You're right. Maybe they can shed some light on these matters and add some pieces to our puzzle. There is one thing I have come to believe over the years and that is that, nothing comes from nothing. One way or the other, there is always a reasonable explanation to any mystery. Our world is too uniquely precise for hocus-pocus theories."

Sam asked Corey to page Ms. Teal. She arrived within minutes and promptly asked; "So, gentlemen and ladies, what have you discovered?"

Buddy took the lead and explained everything the group had previously discussed, including Tooney's drawings of the canyon and the cavern.

Ms. Teal listened with intent while staring at Tooney's sketches. Once Buddy finished with his overview she replied, "It certainly gives us a focal point. Please, keep researching everything you can possibly think of regarding the area where the Ocean Gem got into trouble. Meanwhile, my team is feverishly working on Tooney's formula. Only, we have run into an impasse. Tooney, would you mind coming with me? My advisors are stumped over something regarding your formula and need your advice."

Tooney once more looked up at his mother, she re-assuring him, "You will be okay son; we will be waiting right here."

This time Tooney held out his hand for Chloe to take hold of; she smiled while gently grasping it. Together, they followed Ms. Teal to the waiting sky-tram.

Ms. Teal's group of scientists eagerly greeted Tooney and Chloe when they walked into the New Technologies Lab. The leader, Joseph Hawk, a six foot two inch tall two hundred and sixty pound Sioux Indian stood stoic for a moment, his piercing eyes focusing on Tooney, his expressionless face resembling a block of dark, chiseled granite. His stern glare slowly turned into a warm smile as he began speaking in a deep, sage tone; "You are on the path of an incredible journey."

Tooney, for a moment, could only stare at the floor.

Joseph continued, "Young one, we are calling you 'White Eagle' because of your far-sighted vision and the purity of your heart. Your knowledge is very great and we need your help. Please, teach us. Our promise to you is to use what you share with us only for good." Joseph slowly approached and carefully placed on Tooney's head a turquoise beaded headband with five eagle feathers fanned out across the back.

Chloe remarked, "That is so *awesome.*"

Tooney's grip on Chloe's hand tightened, his eyes rising slowly and locking onto hers. Chloe was beaming with excitement. Tooney then turned to Joseph and nodded his head.

Joseph continued; "Please, young ones, join us in our discovery room."

Tooney and Chloe followed Joseph, Ms. Teal, and their team of scientists into an amazing round room that was some fifty feet in circumference. The center of the room sported a large, round, hickory conference table with twenty built-in, evenly spaced, computer stations. Huge, hi-def, individual monitors lined the perimeter walls directly across the room from each seat, being high enough to prevent blocking the view of the person sitting on the opposite side of the table.

Once seated, Joseph directed everyone's attention to a diagram of the substructure for one particular submersible design. He then spoke; "Young White Eagle, you have shown us something we have never seen before; transparent titanium. We are currently in the process of beginning its production; yet, its weight has us puzzled. Though it is very light and strong, we do not know how to implement its use in a submersible hull design, something that will allow exploration of deep ocean trenches. From our calculations, using solid material in its raw state will apparently require a sub-structure that will be too thick and cumbersome, severely limiting the space necessary for operating the craft. How do we solve this problem?"

Before Tooney could answer, Chloe raised her hand and said, "I can help you with that." She then asked Tooney, "Do you mind if I show them?"

Tooney could not resist yielding to Chloe, seeing a special sparkle in her eyes.

"Tooney taught me the principle of this dynamic only yesterday. It is really quite simple." From her keyboard, she typed in 'geometrical graphics' and, clicking on Open Design, proceeded to produce an image across the screen. The horizontal and vertical lines continued the same pattern repeatedly. She then dropped down a few spaces, duplicating the pattern. "Now, what do these images represent," she asked?

"They represent the Greek symbol for . . . eternity," answered Ms. Teal.

"That is right," agreed Chloe, "because they follow an endless symmetrical pattern. Actually, all matter in the universe follows an infinitely diverse pattern of atomic symmetry. It is common knowledge that atoms are like miniature solar systems; protons and electrons, much like literal planets and moons, surrounding their sun, or nucleus, giving the atom its stability and strength. Because of their 'cosmic precision', we can predict how elements will react with one another when introduced to a variety of conditions. Knowing this helps us put Earth's basics to a variety of uses. We perceive this pattern of unique structure from virtually everything visible in creation. Take for instance, the honeycomb. It appears so vulnerable, so simple; yet when we look at its structure up close, we marvel at its design and complexity. Infinite repetition makes it incredibly strong and reusable multiple times for honey production. Actually, many manufacturing companies use profiles observed in nature to develop their products calling it, bio-mimicry. One company in particular uses the honeycomb design to strengthen its snow skis. Let's make a similar application to our unique Greek symbol for eternity by connecting the lines." Chloe very carefully connected each corner of the top symbol to the corresponding corner of the bottom symbol. "We now have a three dimensional image similar to that of a honeycomb, though . . . uniquely complex. Whether the ancients knew it or not, what appears to be a simple symbolism is, in three-dimensional form, a design dynamic for structural strength. Therefore, I propose using the basics of this pattern in your hull design. Coupled with Tooney's help in establishing the appropriate geometric isomer from his discovery, it can significantly reduce the overall mass of the submersible's sub-structure, subsequently yielding plenty of room for the interior. Even depth to pressure ratios will be irrelevant; the hull will be impervious to collapse at any depth."

Chloe stopped for a moment, running her fingers through her hair and clearing her throat; "Oh, and as a bonus; it will greatly reduce power requirements and absorb sound like a sponge."

Chloe looked at Tooney and whispered, "How was that?"

Tooney stared into her beaming eyes, smiled, and started clapping his hands. All in the room stood up and shared in the applause.

Joseph re-addressed the group with few words: "Please, friends, let's get started."

The production team exited the room quickly, anxious to apply Chloe's idea. Joseph waited, feeling obliged to escort Ms. Teal, Tooney, and Chloe back to Geo-Mapping. Once they arrived, Joseph knelt in front of the two youngsters, holding out both of his hands. They placed their hands on his. He then spoke; "You two are the best of Earth's children. Your inner spirit is not one of competition, but one of unity of purpose. It is no wonder that you comprehend the core simplicity of our world. You are on a successful path." He then stood up, kissed each of them on the forehead, and re-boarded the tram.

Chapter 24

Over the next month, incredible quantities of supplies were arriving on the island via Ms. Teal's private helicopter fleet. The distinctive graphics on the sides of the choppers were of a majestic golden eagle in flight grasping a beautifully colored world globe. The logo beneath it read—'One world, clutched in the talons of wisdom'.

The day finally arrived for all the teams to bring their combined efforts together. Ms. Teal arranged for an island-wide staff meeting, feeling confident that their efforts to explore the unexplainable were now within reach. Over a loud speaker, she addressed the entire population of the island facility, each standing side by side along the banks of the river: "Friends, this is a special day. We are privileged to have in our midst two young people who have revealed to us a unique way to explore the heart of our world. However, what we have learned from them is only scientific. What we have yet to learn is far more fascinating. What we have not yet come to know is . . . why what we perceive to be unintelligible creatures will automatically gravitate toward certain individuals. Master White Eagle's experience with a young dolphin raises many questions, yet excites the hearts of those of us who see this world as a shared experience. This unexplained connection could be the key to unlocking many mysteries. The information we have compiled over the last month from all of our scientific teams, coupled with the hard work of our production crew, has brought us to this exciting moment."

Ms. Teal then reached for a security credential, pushed the button, and in an instant, an amazing, nearly invisible sea craft emerged from beneath the river. The outer shell was hardly detectable with the exception of water rolling off as it ascended. Joleen continued with a description of the vessel: "Friends, you are looking at something that defies our previous, limited understanding of Earth's elements. With the help of young White Eagle and Chloe, we have come to a new understanding of the building blocks of created matter. I present to you the new age of ocean exploration . . . *Nations Pride*."

For a moment, all stood in the grip of silence; but suddenly, the tranquil hush surrendered to thunderous applause. Sam O'Brien and Buddy Gold were stunned, blown away at the speed with which Jolene's staff completed the production of such an incredible vessel in only one month. While its capacity was being further narrated by Joseph Hawk, Sam motioned Joleen away from the group and asked; "I don't understand . . . you never said anything . . . how did you manage this? Why is this project so important to you?"

Joleen looked into his eyes and said, "We did it for you, Sam. Knowing what you went through to save your passengers and crew deserves a special reward. And besides—you are a special man, Sam O'Brien." She then grasped both his hands and, leaning forward, kissed him. In that special moment, Sam experienced a final closure over the death of his dear wife. His heart began surging with excitement over the possibility of a fresh start with someone who could share his life and his dreams. Placing one hand on Sam's chest, Joleen gently pushed away, awaiting his reaction. Sam responded by pulling her tight into his arms and kissing her again, very tenderly. Then staring deep into her vivid blue eyes he stated, "This is terribly sudden; but lady, I think I have fallen in love with you."

Joleen smiled while placing her right index finger on Sam's lips: "We can talk later; right now we have a lot of work to do. Oh, and by the way, we have been working on the ship's design for several years. The only thing we were lacking was what Chloe and Tooney shared with us. I think we are going to make quite a team."

She then stepped back, her hands slowly slipping out of his, and giving him a wink, withdrew to speak with her cousin James. Sam had not noticed Chloe standing only about ten feet away, watching her father's interaction with Ms. Teal. The look on Chloe's face was classic; eyes wide open, her head slightly cocked to one side, her arms and legs crossed, and a crooked little grin on her face as if to say . . . 'now , what was that all about'. Sensing his affection for Ms. Teal met with his daughters approval, Sam could not help himself; he swept Chloe up in his arms and said, "Well, little one, it looks as though we are on track for a whole new adventure."

Chloe clutched her father's face in her hands and with happy tears trickling out of the corners of her eyes said, "Daddy, she is wonderful." She then kissed her dad right on his lips, nuzzled her head tightly between his head and shoulder, hugging him tighter than she had in her entire life.

Chapter 25

During the weeks leading up to the introduction of Nations Pride, Tooney's father had been busy working on a theory of his own. He had a hunch about the timing of the coronal mass ejection off the sun and its hypothetical reaction with the crystal his son claimed he saw. It seemed clear to Charlie that a solar flare did actually trigger the event they observed in the Triangle. His determination now was . . . artificially precipitating the same reaction. As far-fetched as his idea seemed, it was worth discussing. He approached Sam who, after listening to Charlie's analysis, agreed to an audience with Ms. Teal and Joseph Hawk. Ms. Teal arranged for a meeting with all of Sam's associates in the New Technologies Lab.

Charlie began with his observations: "Friends, I have worked most of my life as a mechanical engineer, developing prototypes for extreme altitude, hypersonic aircraft. My employer released me when I put my family's interest ahead of company loyalty. Yet, their action did not keep the wheels in my head from slowing down. At the time of my termination, I was secretly working on a design for an aircraft called a UAV; you no doubt recognize that as an acronym for 'unmanned aerial vehicles'. Now, I am not talking about a drone. The type of aircraft I am talking about is far more advanced. I took the basics of the Lockheed Aurora and merged the design with a Harrier jet. From my perspective, the finished product would be the ultimate spy-plane. It was too fast for having to worry about evasive maneuvers, could fly at altitudes previously impossible for any manned aircraft, and could completely stop in mid flight for high definition photo scanning. With engines powered by hydrogen, I also managed to conceive an exhaust diffusing system, which cycles the vaporous waste before exiting the craft, cooling it significantly; therefore, making it undetectable to heat sensing devices. My final intention was to attach a weapons grade laser beneath it. I actually completed the design of, what I call—a light infusion laser. It is as close to an anti-matter weapon as has ever existed. Its initial impact injects a target with an intense ray of light, causing a chaotic chain-reaction within the targeted object, imploding its atomic structure. The target does not completely disappear; it just shrinks to about one billionth of its original size. I never shared my inventions with anyone, knowing that if they ever fell into the hands of the military or some rogue nation, the consequences could be lethal for the entire world. However, over the past few weeks, I have been thinking about my son's description of the crystal, which by now we all feel had something to do with the fiery phenomena that gripped the Ocean Gem and almost drug her down. This new aircraft design, coupled with an adjustment to the laser's intensity, could be a way to duplicate a solar event. Tooney and I can work together to modify and test the beam: after all, the last thing we want to see happen to the crystal is—watching it disappear."

All in the room remained quiet for several moments, contemplating Charlie's comments. Buddy Gold finally spoke up: "As long as we are on the subject, I have something to add. I cannot go into lengthy details—I can only say that my colleagues and I are in possession of a Lockheed Aurora. We have been trying to re-design its capacity for high altitude reef imagery, which would help us monitor the effects of pollution, climate change, and natural disasters at far greater speed and efficiency than ever before imagined. Our activity, though, is highly classified. The U.S. Government has an oversight committee that checks up on us every six months to track our progress. Charlie's idea on the Aurora's re-design sounds exactly like what we have been trying to accomplish.

Of course, we were thinking along the lines of equipping it with only a camera, not a laser.

Sam, Ms. Teal, and Joseph Hawk had the same look in their eyes, their heads nodding with approval at what Buddy was apparently offering for their use; the aircraft. Joleen glanced over at her cousin James with a look that begged for his full co-operation. James replied with a simple nod.

Joseph Hawk decided it would be a good time to make Charlie, Carlynn, Tooney, and Chloe a part of their New Technologies design team. James Powell accepted the task of security operations manager for the island, while Sam, Corey, and Buddy took full control of Nations Pride project operations.

Chapter 26

Socrates and his friends were working diligently on their plan to free the hostages. The mission was going to be dangerous with no way of calculating real time. They simply had to rely on observing the repetitive schedules of the humans along the shoreline. Kooks managed a communication break-through when she had Java try to send a message to Socrates from her remote location on the other side of the bay. Jibber, Stony, and Rocky all heard the sonic transmission and hurriedly sought out Socrates. "What did she say," he asked excitedly.

"No, you first," Jibber insisted; "Who is she?"

"Only the prettiest dolphin I've ever seen," Socrates replied. "Her name is Java; she is Kooks' friend who, like us, traversed one of the dimensional windows during a solar event, stranding them in an area on the other side of this bay. Now, what did she say?"

"She said they have figured out a way to open the web at a point near a terraced rock wall that comes down to the water's edge. It is close to where the female human is bringing the captives and helping them."

"Okay, that is good," replied Socrates. "Go back and let her know that we received the message and to stay sharp; we are close to putting our plan into action."

Jibber sped off to send the reply. Barely a minute had passed when Java responded; "Peetie has everything figured out and ready to go. When the excitement begins, he wants you dolphins to speed to the back of the bay. On your signal, I will transmit directions to our exact location."

Jibber quickly relayed this information to Socrates who rounded up all the participants, reviewing every phase of their plan. Timing and precision was critical because of the extreme danger. With all the details complete, the time arrived for the operation to begin.

Kabooga waited quietly at a watch-point for the procession of evil humans to gather in front of the column housing the small meteorite. The pompous leader, his head wrapped high and tight in seaweed, began his routine procedure of leading the procession in bowing and chanting before the column.

Next, they started filing past and kissing the small jagged object inside. Kabooga was trying hard not to laugh; it all seemed ridiculous to him. As soon as the humans vacated the area, Uncle Gnarls motioned for the octopus to proceed. Kabooga gently raised one of his giant tentacles out of the water, plucking the meteorite from its support. He then carefully replaced it with a large snapper-clam, which he had been clutching tight in another of his tentacles to avoid it springing open. With this part of the plan accomplished, he quietly submerged. There was nothing left to do except to wait for the humans to return.

Socrates' friends were intently focusing on the ensuing battle, realizing they were going to be in mortal danger by either the evil humans or the terrifying crocs and pterodactyls. Yet, with each passing moment, they were becoming more emboldened to see this fight through to a finish. They began challenging one another, moving around at top speed, practicing their evasive maneuvers, hoping it would be enough to equip them for the impending danger. Gnarls finally signaled the humans' arrival, an eerie silence gripping the bay.

Once again, the procession followed its usual procedure when suddenly, one of the humans shouted and pointed at the column. Rushing over, their leader stared at the object inside, and then turned with his arms extended, shouting something at the top of his lungs. The humans started jumping up and down, joyfully chanting with tears running down their faces as though there had been some kind of magical change to the meteorite. Socrates motioned to NuiMalu, Mau, Ka'e'a'e'a, Serine, and Zippee to round up the crocs. They quickly sped away.

It took only a brief moment to get the crocs attention. Nui mimicked the shriek of an injured plesiosaur and began flapping around on the surface. The crocs came storming out of their lair. Nui hurried off while Serine and Zippee streaked forward, darting in and out of the group of horrifying creatures, stirring them up. The crocs were going crazy trying to target the two speedsters, but to no avail; Serine and Zippee were too fast for the huge beasts. The crocs finally slowed for a moment, their energy briefly expended; that is when Mau gave the signal for the girls to begin a trek back to the bay. The enraged crocs took off after them. Now it was Mau, Ka'e'a'e'a, and Nui's turn to stir up the action. Coming out of hiding, the plesiosaurs swept in from behind, head slapping a few of the beasts before bolting after Serine and Zippee. The crocs went ballistic, their mouths opening wide, their heads slashing wildly back and forth, their fiery eyes blazing with anger, speeding after their antagonizers in a crazed fury. At the entrance to the bay, Serine and Zippee peeled off while the plesiosaurs started breaching in and out of the water. Pterodactyls, noticing the commotion, began dropping off their high perches, swooshing in low and gliding over the surface of the water.

The evil human leader must have thought this was some sort of sign and turned back toward the column, bending over to kiss the object inside. The clams shell sprang open, revealing its beautiful interior. Stricken with awe, the man began lightly stroking the colorful inner surface, smiling with intrigue as though the object gave him justification as leader. The man's smile quickly faded when the clams' jagged shell suddenly slammed shut, snapping his wrist. He ran wildly in a circle, screaming for help. The other humans were trying to help pry the thing off, but to no avail. The man then ran to the water's edge, sticking his hand in, hoping the clam would let go. Locking on to his silhouette, one of the crocs lunged forward, plucking the man off the ledge, consuming the evil cleric in a single bite. All that remained was the seaweed head-wrap that once identified him as leader. The battle was now on.

Brandishing their spears, the humans started hurling them at the armored beasts who were aggressively trying to climb the walls of the bay. Targeting the flying creatures, the plesiosaurs started plucking them out of the sky as they swept in low over the surface of the bay. Some of the crocs retreated from pursuing the humans to take advantage of the avian beasts flailing in the water, their circumstance making them an easy meal. What the crocs did not realize was . . . what was now in store for them. Large, vicious, electric eels in numbers beyond comprehension started swarming the surface. Three of the crocs opened their mouths wide, targeting a tight mass of the slimy carrion feeders. The resulting contact was more than they bargained for. The intense voltage fried the crocs brains in an instant. The bay was now involved in a huge free for all. It was a perfect time for the dolphins to get to the back of the bay. Speeding away, Jibber communicated to Java the need for directions to the location she alluded to earlier. The dolphins held their breath as long as they could but the second they broke the surface for air, spears pierced the water, and one of the crocs took off after them. The dolphins were now in a predicament; they could not compromise the location at the back of the bay where the lone woman was attending the captives. Stony and Rocky noticed the gape of a gigantic clam embedded in the reef whose shell was at least thirty feet across. Rocky slowed to get the full attention of the croc while Stony dove straight for the bottom. Rocky toyed with the crazed reptile, swimming in circles and jabbing its underbelly. With a signal from Stony, Rocky lured the beast into what looked like an entry to a cave. Rocky sped through with the croc following within inches of his tail. That is when Stony swept in from above, dropping an old piece of jagged coral down into the meaty interior of the clam, causing an abrupt reaction. Stony and Rocky escaped just in time, but the croc never made it. Upon hearing a horrific cracking sound, the dolphins turned . . . only to see the monster's head hanging out of one end of the clam's shell, the tip of its tail out the other, its body remaining trapped inside and unable to move, its spinal cord severed under the crushing force of the ancient mollusks' carapace.

Stony cried out, "They don't call us Stony and Rocky for nothing!" The two slapped each other's fin and took off, re-joining Jibber and Schooner.

Back in the bay, the ferocity of the battle continued intensifying, the human captors fighting off the advances of the crocs and pterodactyls. The numbers of the pre-historic beasts were diminishing, the humans suffering quite a few casualties of their own. In the course of the fight, one of the crocs managed to climb onto the rock mass in front of the worship column and, with a slash of its tail, knocked about twenty of the humans into the water. On the shore, it targeted one lone individual. The man backed up to the wall of a cliff, completely trapped, the monster inching forward, teasing its prey. Unexpectedly, a lone captive appeared, and grabbing a spear, ran forward. The captor thought the man was going to run him through as repayment for having suffered timeless abuse. To the captor's surprise, the slave threw a stone at the beast to get its attention. When the croc spun around, the slave thrust the spear with all his might into its wide-open mouth, the spearhead entering the back of its throat and exiting below the first row of curled armor on its back. The beast's eyes rolled, its tail slashing violently back and forth, finally falling limp and sliding back into the water. The captor stared at the slave in wonderment. The slave yelled out; "What do you not understand? We were *never* your enemies! Your leader lied to you! All these years, *you* have been his slaves! Right now, your only enemies are the monsters in the water and the pterodactyls; and from the looks of things, the battle is close to a finish! Come on, grab a spear, we can finish them off!"

The captor wavered for a moment, hanging his head in shame, sickened by the thought of his having been deceived by a charismatic maniac who haughtily strutted around with seaweed draped around his head. Snapping out of his stupor, he energetically picked up a spear, following the slave to the water's edge. In his desperation to seek a position of advantage, the slave lost his footing and, slipping on the wet surface, tumbled off the ledge and into the water. Another croc moved in quickly for the kill. Shredder and Jacko were close by and responded immediately by ramming the beast to divert its attention away from the victim while Poker, carrying one of the spears sideways in his bill, raced in towards the croc at full speed, its razor sharp fangs glistening and dripping with blood. At the last second, Poker turned sideways, charging right into the beasts' stretched-open jaws and wedging the spear vertically in the back of its throat. The creature instinctively bit down hard only to send the spear tip through its brain, killing it instantly. Serine screamed, *"Poker, No-o-o-o-o."*

Poker, squirming his way out and bleeding from contact with the croc's sharp teeth, finally managed to call out, *"I'm okay!"*

The slave quickly swam back toward the ledge. The captor stood on the edge of the rock mass, stunned, and motionless, having witnessed the fish coming to the rescue of the man in the water. Before climbing the ledge, the slave turned, only to catch Poker giving him a wink and then disappearing. The captor quickly helped the slave out of the water, both men scurrying back up the rocky bluff. They noticed one last croc targeting more of the humans in the water. This time Kabooga re-emerged from the depths and, grabbing the monster, rolled it up tight in one of his gigantic, fifty-foot long tentacles. He then lifted it out of the water and threw it hard into the side of a cliff, the impact causing a massive landslide, crushing the horrible beast in its wake. The slave took no chances; he ran over and plunged a spear through the crocs' eye, pushing it in hard and piercing its brain. Kabooga's head slowly emerged just below the water line, training his eyes on the men, the captor shaking, scared out of his wits. Kabooga slowly raised another of his tentacles, the one clutching the small meteorite, and hurled the infernal thing hard into the remaining cliff face, shattering it into a million pieces. He then extended the huge appendage toward the frightened captor and, with the tip, gently stroked the terrified man's face. With that, Kabooga withdrew, disappearing from sight.

The fight was finally over, the remaining eels interested only in gorging themselves on sinking carcasses.

The slave stood silent for a moment, shocked at what just happened. He approached the captor who was still trembling, grabbed him by his shoulders, and looking him in the eyes said; "You have never called me by my name! My name is Ben, Ben Steel! It is time to stop this nonsense and work together!" Ben then took off running to the back of the bay where the rest of the captives were hiding. The beautiful woman who had been helping them embraced Ben when he returned.

Seeing the battle complete, Socrates and Uncle Gnarls instructed all their friends to hurry to the back of the bay. When they arrived, the captives were lining the shore, the dolphins entertaining them with a jumping display. The dolphins were simply trying to coax the humans to follow them to the web. Out of sheer terror, the captives cowered in fear when the plesiosaurs arrived. Only Ben, who was involved in the battle, was willing to approach the magnificent creatures. Ka'e'a'e'a started swimming toward him, extending his head beneath Bens' outreached hands. Ben responded by climbing onto the plesiosaur's neck, triumphantly cruising through the pristine water, the captives cheering his victory. This gave Socrates an idea. He swam alongside Ka'e'a'e'a: "Follow Schooner to the opening in the web."

Ka'e'a'e'a began submerging alongside Schooner who, following Java's sonic chirps, found the opening. There to greet them was none other than Peetie, with a huge smile on his face, motioning to bring the man forward. Ben spotted the opening, let go of his ride, and swam through. After a very short distance, his head emerged above the waterline into a beautiful cavern. He looked around for a moment and noticed a large archway on one side. He swam through it and gasped at what he saw. The enormous bay sported an exotic landscape of trees, waterfalls, and creatures of every sort. Colorful birds were flitting around while small animals played along the water's edge. This was the most beautiful and peaceful place he had ever seen. He quickly swam back into the cavern, retreating through the web. Re-emerging, he motioned excitedly for all to follow him. The captives were reluctant, still a bit frightened. Noticing their hesitation, Stony, Rocky, and Jibber lined up at the water's edge, enticing them to hop on for a ride. The beautiful woman, Malanai, perceiving the dolphins' intentions, dove into the water, and grabbing on to Stony's dorsal fin, sped away, her laughter splitting the air with excitement. All the captives now joined her in the water. Socrates and his friends swam around, frolicking, jumping, and splashing. This playful diversion helped Ben to lure the captives, one by one, to the opening in the web. It took some time; however, all the captives, as well as the fish, were finally safe. With their mission complete, the plesiosaurs then reversed course for their trek to the bay via the opposite direction.

Exiting the water onto a beautiful sandy beach, Ben and Malanai took the lead in getting the captives settled in. Socrates and his friends were thrilled to be re-uniting with Two Stars, Noni, and the rest of their group.

Little Peetie was so proud to have accomplished such a feat as creating the opening in the web. With his head held high, he announced, "Follow me, and observe, please, a master weaver's work."

The little rockfish called for Kaimana, Shredder, and Schooner. Kaimana had previously helped Peetie to gather a large mass of tube kelp from the outreaches of the bay. Together they braided the tubes to strengthen them. They then fastened the kelp around two adjacent vertical strands of the web. To the other end of each length of kelp, they formed a loop, attaching it to a sharp point on the outer lip of two monstrous clams with shells gaped open and growing in the reef close to opposing outer edges of the web. Opening the web had been easy. Kaimana simply dropped a jagged piece of dead coral down into the clams' meaty interiors. When the clams' shells suddenly closed, the strands of the web stretched open. Now, with everyone safely through, and Peetie's description of his masterpiece fully disclosed, he ordered: "*Shredder*, bite through that length of kelp!"

Shredder raced over to one side and in one crushing bite, the kelp snapped, closing half of the opening. Peetie, Schooner, and Kaimana raced to the other clam and simply tapped on its outer shell. The shell sprung wide open and the other side of the web returned to its original position. Peetie and Schooner then gently slid the noose off the sharp point of the clam. "Now, is that awesome or what," Peetie gloated?

All the fish began applauding, telling Peetie what a genius he is. For a moment, he sucked up all the accolades, but unexpectedly, he slumped in sadness and started sobbing. Socrates and Amaya swam over to him: "What's up, little guy?"

"I only wish Bondar were here to see it. I really miss him. Do you think he would be . . . proud of me?"

"Are you kidding," answered Amaya, "by the time this adventure is over you will be the most famous rockfish in the entire ocean. Bondar is going to be brimming with pride over his son."

The little rockfish's face took on a surprised glare; "Did you say . . . son?"

"Yes, Peetie . . . Bondar told me one day before we got into this mess that he feels more like your father than just a friend. Believe me, little one, when he hears about this he is going to be very proud. By the way, why did you have Shredder bite through the kelp on one end when all you had to do was simply tap on the clams shell to get it to open?

Peetie looked around and, motioning the two away from the rest of the fish, he whispered; "Well, I got to thinking that by including him we might restore a little of his dignity. He has seemed awfully depressed lately, having gotten us into this predicament."

"That is true," replied Amaya, "yet, look how it all worked out; if it had not been for his ill-conceived action, how much longer would these poor captives be terrorized? I think it is time for the three of us to give him a little pep talk; what do you say?"

Peetie smiled and replied, "Right now seems like a good time for that. "

Chapter 27

Ms. Teal and her teams of scientists were working diligently on their plan for exploring the canyon. The strides they made in just a few weeks were legendary. Outfitted with all the proper equipment, Nations Pride successfully completed several deep ocean runs in and around naval destroyers and submarines without detection. The vessel could cruise underwater at sixty knots and maneuver like a fighter jet. Her engines were pure genius. They were hydrogen powered and fitted with a liquefying exhaust system that turned the gaseous expulsion into water. The water then channeled through a separator, causing it to fan out and build up pressure through funneled-down exhaust ports. The ports were located on all four sides with hydraulic titanium scuppers sealing them closed until propulsion in one particular direction was necessary. Once expelled, the water yielded no bubbles, no sound, just pure acceleration.

A liquid titanium casement sealed the instrument panels, making them impervious to conditions interference. In addition, Charlie's reconstruction of the Aurora proved a masterpiece. With an intense sense of pride, he renamed it . . . 'Raptor'. Its cruising altitude within the stratosphere was unlimited with an approximate maximum speed of mach 30. Obtaining this incredible speed within' earth's atmosphere was tricky. The aircraft's re-design was in the shape of a traditional arrowhead coated with a smooth, extreme velocity, non-combustible ceramic. Its curved, bumpy, outer edges mimicked the unusual foreside of humpback whales flippers, forcing an increase in lift and reducing drag. Air would then accelerate over the craft in a rotating flow, literally splitting the atmosphere and breaking apart the gaseous molecules that cause high velocity foreign objects, such as meteorites, to burn up once passing through Earth's orbit. Swiveling thrusters built into its underbelly and tail section, accomplished an almost instantaneous vertical takeoff. Three consecutive test flights over Washington D. C., Moscow, and Beijing, without detection, proved its stealth capability. Cuba was Buddy Gold's choice for the initial laser test. A 1956 Chevy parked on the side of a road would be the target. With one blast from Charlie's original laser, the automobile simply disappeared into thin air. Had the Cuban's had the technology to investigate the disappearance, they would have discovered a vehicle the size of a one-celled organism. Knowing for a certainty the laser's capacity, Charlie and Tooney re-defined its intensity. The laser's power source was the sun. When the Raptor stopped in mid-flight, a special covering retracted from the roof of the craft revealing an enormous, multi-faceted, tapered diamond. The top of the gem was smooth and concave while the opposite end tapered to a needlepoint. The captured light from the sun intensified a million-fold, the diamond narrowing the luminary's nuclear rays. The beam created entered a secondary, inner-faceted, orbital chamber, triggering a hyperactive reaction to its pattern of atoms and molecules, thus causing the emission of a quasar-like, blue light through a tiny, convex window located on the underside, the light's focused impact reducing its target to subatomic proportions. Tooney's idea was to modify the tip of the diamond from a needlepoint to a hexagonal faceted cone, thus widening the intense ray before entering the chamber. This would reduce the laser's reaction on a target by enlarging the beam at point of impact from an original three feet to twenty feet in diameter. Firing the laser from sixty seven thousand feet in altitude, an average target would not disappear; it would however, absorb enough light to glow like the sun. The only problem was; on what do they test the new beam? Chloe came up with a clever idea: "Say, we have all heard news reports about the nuclear ambitions of Iran and North Korea. Why don't we give them a little scare?"

"Wait a minute sweetie," came back Sam, "that could trigger an international incident?"

"Not if they can't identify the source," replied Chloe. "It will look as though they messed something up and will have no one to blame but themselves. The media coverage will be hysterical."

Sam, Joleen, and the entire team shrugged their shoulders and chuckled. After all, what better way could there be to slow nuclear proliferation than to scare the daylights out of the offending nations leaders?

Just before sundown on the following evening, the Raptor raced undetected across the sky and came to a sudden, mid-flight stop over a facility just east of Pyongyang. The laser fired, targeting a radar detection vehicle at a remote site, causing the entire region for several hundred miles to light up like a planetary explosion of phosphorous. Even though there was no damage to anything, the entire population of North Korea thought the world had ended.

The aircraft then streaked away west, and in only about twenty minutes conducted a similar test over an area south of Tehran. Little did Sam's team know that a six point eight-magnitude earthquake hit the same region within the previous three minutes. Once again, the population of the country panicked, fearing their leaders' lack of foresight triggered an uncontrolled nuclear explosion. Media coverage of both incidents instantly flooded the airwaves and the internet, sending the entire world into panic. Yet, with no viable cause of the intense light available to the populace, the only real harm was the humiliation caused to the leaders of the rogue nations because of their lack of an explanation to the public. There was literally no damage, no one injured, and no one to blame.

All the residents of Joleen Teal's private island watched the news coverage for at least two hours following the Raptor's tests. None of them could have known the effect it would have on the world as a whole. Global media coverage obviously scared people. Reports started flooding in about renewing peace treaties and international co-operation. Sam O'Brien just rolled his eyes and commented: "Oh, yeah, sure, and that will last all of what, maybe . . . twenty minutes?"

Joleen laughed and added, "Well, at least long enough for their leaders 'small-man syndrome' to kick back in. That might take only . . . nineteen minutes."

Joleen's entire staff started chuckling and congratulating Chloe for her choice of targets. International attention would now be focusing far away from the area Nations Pride would be exploring.

With its outfitting and testing complete, the ship and its crew were now ready for their first official adventure. Sam and Corey stood ready at the helm while Joleen, Carlynn, Chloe, James, and Joseph examined a checklist of onboard operational procedures. The islands' residents stood by the banks of the river with heads held high, extremely proud of their accomplishments. Buddy, Charlie, and Tooney entered a special control room aboard the sea-craft, making their final preparations for the Raptor's next UAV flight via a remote panel operated aboard ship. The moment to start the exploration finally arrived and the one hundred-foot craft silently submerged and disappeared, proceeding through a subterranean canal into the ocean. Sam marveled at the ease of the craft's mobility and silence. Even the most sophisticated military listening devices could not detect its presence. Yet, every other craft within a hundred miles was clearly discernable to Nations Prides' hi-def monitors. No one on board questioned the pre-programmed co-ordinates to the canyon because Tooney logged them in using his unique understanding of planetary matrix vectors. Chloe was the only other person on board with even a clue of how he did it.

All settled in to their individual tasks, beginning the twelve-hour trek to the canyon.

Chapter 28

Bondar and Big Jake were languishing over their inability to do anything that would help get Socrates and the others back. They could not conceive of any plan with the exception of re-exploring the caverns for clues and keeping order in Amaya's kingdom. Interestingly, the newcomers, Jazzy and Baaya, were making many new friends, everyone loving their zaniness . . . always singing, dancing, and displaying a little attitude. Bondar and Big Jake were getting used to the two young ones hanging out with them, the girls' antics taking the edge off the anxiety everyone was feeling over the mysterious disappearance of Socrates and his friends. However, Jazzy was becoming a bit obsessed over solving the mystery and she and Baaya finally took up residence in the cavern where Socrates and his friends disappeared. They daily made the trek from the cavern to the canyon and back, trying to piece together Bondar's explanation of the strange light causing fire to dance across the surface of the water. Bondar really did appreciate their interest in the search because even Big Jake was getting bored playing the waiting game. He was beginning to think that the search was a lost cause. Bondar could see he was antsy to continue his northerly migration. Neither of them could have known the events that were going to unfold on one particular day.

Jazzy and Baaya were busy with their new routine of examining the areas where all the previous events occurred. As usual, they were singing and swaying to Baaya's favorite songs while checking out every inch of the region. They were approaching the canyon when suddenly Baaya started shouting: *"Whoa, what is happening? Help me!"*

"What are you doing," replied Jazzy, watching Baaya tumbling uncontrollably; "If that's a new dance move, it's a bit spastic don't you think?"

"S-S-S-Something h-h-has a h-h-hold of me!"

"What are you talking about, there is nothing here?"

However, Jazzy caught a glimpse of a large, near—transparent, movement. "What is that?"

"I-I-I have no idea, but it is kn-kn-kn-knocking the d-d-d-daylights out of m-m-m-me! Please Jazzy, h-h-h-help me!"

Baaya finally stopped tumbling, sobbing out of sheer fright. Jazzy hurried her over to the safety of a rock formation.

"Jazzy, I am so scared! What is happening?"

"I don't know, but it seems to be gone now. No, no, there it is; it is heading toward the canyon. *Quick*, let's find Bondar and Big Jake!"

The two young ones explanation of what had happened caused Bondar and Big Jake to roll their eyes a little, thinking the girls were starting to see things. Yet, there was one thing Bondar learned from Socrates that stuck with him from day to day; never ignore good intentions. The improbable can and will frequently surprise you. He and Jake graciously followed Jazzy and Baaya to the rim of the canyon.

Once they arrived Jazzy said, "I just know that it was headed this direction!"

Suddenly, Bondar felt a slight impulse from receptors on the top of his head. Something was definitely in their vicinity, but nothing was visible.

The four carefully scanned the rim of the canyon. "Where is it," asked Bondar? "Something is definitely here, I can feel it. This is crazy!"

Baaya suddenly froze and stammered: "H-H-H-Hey guys; look up!"

The surface of the water split from a nearly invisible craft breaking the surface. Water cascaded off it as it ascended above the center of the canyon. Neither of the fish had ever seen anything like it. The craft was easily twice the length of Big Jake, completely silent, and eerily transparent.

"What do you think it is," asked Jazzy?

"I have no idea," replied Bondar, "but we are staying right here until we figure it out."

"Look," shouted Baaya, "something is opening on the top!"

Bondar freaked when Tooney's head popped up: *"It's him,"* cried Bondar, *"it's the little boy that Schooner saved! He's come back!"*

"Are you sure that's him," asked Baaya.

"Oh yeah . . . it's him; *Check this out.*"

Bondar approached the craft and stuck his head out of the water directly in front of Tooney. The little boys' eyes grew wide when Bondar winked at him. Impulsively, Tooney climbed completely out of the hatch, ran to the stern, and plunged into the ocean. The ship's crew panicked, scrambling to the deck and screaming. Bondar swam beneath the little guy, raising him to the surface on his back. Tooney boldly called out, "I'm the ruler of the sea. Who dares mess with me?"

Bondar was ecstatic over re-uniting with this little person. He gleefully swam in circles around the craft for a few minutes before bringing Tooney to the outreached arms of the Captain. Chloe started hyperventilating from the overwhelming emotion of seeing Tooney's special relationship with the huge hammerhead. Tooney's parents, as well as the rest of the team, looked as if their minds were experiencing a surrealistic dream. Sam O'Brien however, was not surprised, knowing the shark was in some way linked to the incredible mystery surrounding the canyon.

Bondar motioned for Jazzy, Baaya, and Big Jake to come closer to the craft. "Okay, Jake, stay on the surface and slowly circle the craft. Jazzy and Baaya, do your thing."

"You mean like singing and dancing," came back Jazzy? "What is that going to accomplish?"

"Call it a hunch," replied Bondar; "But for some reason I think our connection with the little boy is going to help us."

"Whatever," replied Jazzy? "Okay Baaya, hit it."

Baaya busted out in song while Jazzy started swaying to the music and emphasizing the beat through the motion of her fins and tail.

Chloe blurted out, "Look at that other shark; It looks like it's—dancing." Chloe actually started moving to Jazzys' rhythmic gyrations.

Joseph Hawk and Joleen Teal stood side by side, clutching each other's hand and watching in silence, feeling a certain cultural inspiration over the strange connection between these young ones and the fish in the water. However, a voice quickly broke the silence: *"Captain, hurry,"* shouted Corey Coulson! *"You have got to see this!"*

Sam scurried back down the hatch. "Captain, look at the screen!"

Sam gawked at the image Corey had zoomed in on and displayed on the hi-def screen. A huge diamond crystal, supported by columns of gold sat on the bottom of the canyon directly below Nations Pride. Sam called to Buddy to get everyone below.

"But, dad, what about the fish," cried out Chloe?

"I'm sure they will hang around sweetheart. Right now we need to focus on what we came here for."

Chloe rolled her eyes, her shoulders slumping from disappointment, reluctantly submitting to her father's request. Joseph Hawk smiled at her reaction and, placing his hand on her back, stooped over and whispered; "My heart tells me you are going to get more time with the fish."

Chloe gave Joseph a ho-hum smile and a lazy high five, hoping he was right.

The hatch on Nations Pride quickly closed and the craft re-submerged, heading straight down the throat of the canyon.

"Well, what do we do now . . . *huuuuh*," asked Baaya in a snooty little tone?

Bondar replied, "don't let it get to you little one, not everyone likes that song."

Baaya was stunned at Bondar's words; of course, he was only kidding. Jazzy started laughing at the look on Baaya's face. "Oh, c'mon Baaya, lighten up; Bondar was just pulling your fin."

"Yeah, well, perhaps he should keep his remarks to himself," Baaya replied.

Jake was snickering over the conversation and offered an idea: "Say Bondar, why don't you and Jazzy follow the craft to the bottom and I will keep Baaya occupied until you return."

"And what do you propose we do, hmm," asked Baaya, "just hang out and watch while they have all the fun?"

Big Jake smiled, "you want fun, I will show you fun. See that big hole in my fluke: swim under it and poke your head through."

Baaya curiously made her way down the length of Big Jake's mammoth body and under his fluke. Upon seeing her head pop up through the hole, Jake pushed his fluke down hard, shooting Baaya into the sky like a rocket. "*Whoa,*" she screamed as she soared upward toward an endless firmament streaked with lacy clouds. Her descent was equally spectacular, she tucking her head and re-entering the water in a perfect dive: "Now, that's what I'm talking about! Please, please, please, can we do it again?"

Big Jake smiled, "We can do it all day long if you wish. I am in no hurry to go anywhere."

Baaya ecstatically sped back for another blast into the sky.

Bondar looked at Jake and said, "Thanks buddy, I owe you one. Hopefully we won't be too long; I have an idea on how to get them to follow us to the cavern."

With that, Bondar and Jazzy turned to follow the almost undetectable craft.

"So what is your plan," asked Jazzy?

"My first idea is to see how much of the canyon they explore before resurfacing. If they seem to miss anything, you and I are going to bring it to their attention."

"And how do you propose we do that?"

"Oh, I think we might just use a little method Two-Stars taught us." Then smiling he added, "If it becomes necessary, I will let you know."

Jazzy stopped for a moment, glaring at Bondar; feeling annoyed at his chopped response. She finally shrugged it off and followed him into the canyon's depths.

A cold wave of stunned silence gripped the crew of Nations Pride as it descended, the scattered remains of at least a dozen huge ships coming into view. Joleen Teal broke the silence in a trembling whisper: "Oh, Sam, this is *eerie*. This is a . . . *graveyard*."

"Yeah," he replied, "and it was almost the final resting place of the Ocean Gem and everyone onboard." A sudden shiver rolled up his spine and tears started welling up in his eyes.

Joleen put her arms around him and said, "I am beginning to sense the terror you must have felt. But what can explain the force pulling the ship down?"

Corey blurted out, "Captain, look portside about ten o'clock! What do you make of that?"

Sam looked up and saw the remains of several planes hanging vertically some one hundred feet above the canyon floor. "I don't understand," replied Sam, "what keeps them from plunging to the bottom?"

Tooney spoke up and simply stated, "Magnetism."

"Yeah, but what—how?" Sam could not even finish his sentence because nothing here made any sense.

As the craft made its way around the perimeter of the canyon Buddy noticed something else unusual: "Look at the crystal panels lining the wall over there. What do you suppose they are for?"

The attention of the entire staff turned to Tooney.

Tooney felt a little embarrassed and grasped his mother's hand. Carlynn reassured him: "It's okay son, no one is pressuring you; it's just that you seem to know more about this than anyone. We are just fishing for answers."

Tooney smiled at Chloe whose eyes were still as big as saucers over everything she had seen so far. He then said, "They spread light through the caverns."

"What caverns, Tooney? Where are the caverns," asked the Captain?

"Follow the shark, he knows."

James Powell, whose words had remained few since the beginning of this expedition, finally offered: "Sam, listen to him. Clues are only as good as their source and . . . you *know* Tooney. Follow his lead."

Sam had no problem accepting James' suggestion.

"Tooney," Sam asked, "how do we find the shark?"

"Look aft."

Corey immediately brought the images from the stern camera up on the big screen and sure enough, Bondar and Jazzy were within twenty feet of the ship.

Corey asked, "How would you suggest we enlist their help Captain?"

Sam thought for a moment then replied; "Do we have any way of projecting an image onto one of those panels lining the canyon wall?"

"Yes sir," Corey replied, "what do you have in mind?"

The Captain never had a chance to answer; Tooney moved over next to Corey, rolled up his sleeve, and acted as if he were pushing his hand through something.

Remembering Tooney's previous explanation of the wavy window, Corey caught on immediately: "Good idea Tooney, let's hope this works."

Corey had Tooney repeat his action, scanning his motion into a digital imagery projector. He then fired the video into one of the crystal panels.

Bondar responded immediately: "There is our answer Jazzy; I think the little guy is sending us a message. Let's get out of here and head toward the cavern!"

The two sharks began their slow accent back to the surface with Nations Pride following close behind.

"I sure hope someone is documenting all of this," Ms. Teal commented.

"Everything and every word Ms. Teal," came back Corey, "This is going to make a great movie."

"Hey," shouted James, "You are treading on dangerous ground young man!"

"Yeah, yeah, I know," came back Corey, "everything is *classified*. But that doesn't mean *we* can't watch it, does it?"

James glared at Corey with a half threatening look, pointing his index finger at the young first mate, then two fingers back at his own eyes, repeating the motion a couple of times indicating, "I've got my eyes on you." Corey turned back to Sam O'Brien, winked and stated in a playful, sarcastic tone of voice, "Continuing our *classified* mission back to the surface Captain. Shall I . . . sound the alarm?"

Agent Powell rolled his eyes while the rest of the crew chuckled at Corey's improv.

Once the craft crested the top of the canyon, Bondar and Jazzy found Baaya and Big Jake waiting for them. Baaya was so excited; in the short time she spent with him, she came to love the one whom she now considered her hero; Big Jake. "I want to stay forever," she shared with Jazzy. "I really love it here. Do you think they will make us leave when this is all over?"

Bondar overheard the conversation and replied, "Are you kidding? Without your attitude, things would get very boring around here. You are definitely staying. After all, someone has to keep Jake occupied and out of trouble."

Jazzy and Baayas' smiles grew wide; together they were experiencing an overwhelming feeling of acceptance. The two paused for a moment, giving each other a little hug. They then got in line to follow Bondar and Big Jake to the cavern.

While recording the actions of the fish Corey Coulson gasped for a moment: "Captain, did you see that? Did the tiger shark give that angelfish a . . . hug?"

"Do not ask Seaman Coulson, just follow and record. I am sure we are in for a lot of surprises down here."

Chapter 29

"Captain, quick, you have to see this!"

Corey Coulson was an individual who prided himself on absorbing his surroundings and keeping a sharp eye out for the unusual. His captain responded immediately: "What is it?"

"Sir, look at the monitor. Look at how clear the water is in this area."

"Yeah, it is amazingly clear; so what?"

"What else do you see besides the fish we are following?"

The Captain scanned the entire area that was visible to the cameras lining the hull of Nations Pride. Besides the four fish ahead of them, he saw nothing. "Okay, what do you see that I don't?"

"Nothing, Sir, I see absolutely nothing; that is precisely the point. Except for those we are following, the entire area is devoid of fish. Now, notice the ocean floor; there is hardly any sand. Our mineral scanners are reading the bottom as being eighty percent metallic. I examined our computer log a moment ago and it shows we have been over this metallic zone for the last one hundred miles. What do you make of it, Sir?"

Captain O'Brien began stroking his chin, his mind racing with ideas. Only one made sense. He noticed the rest of the crew busy with other things so he simply bent forward, whispering to Corey, "Keep these stats under your hat for awhile. Our immediate task is to find the cavern."

"You got it, Skipper."

Sam turned and started walking away from the screen when Corey quickly grabbed the back of Sam's shirt: "Captain, look!"

Sam's eyes narrowed as he viewed Bondar, Jazzy, and Baaya entering a large, conical shaped corridor jutting up from the ocean floor. Big Jake suddenly breached completely out of the water right in front of Nations Pride, forcing Corey to slam his thrusters in reverse, bringing the craft to a sudden halt.

The quick stop brought the entire crew running forward to see what happened. The Captain's eyes focused on the shape of the entry to the corridor: "What in the world is that?"

Ms. Teal spoke up; "The shape looks like the lip of a giant queen conch."

"Yeah, well," replied Corey, "there is no way this vessel will fit into that small of an entry."

"That's okay," replied the Captain, "I think we have reached our destination. Buddy, Joleen, Charlie . . . grab your scuba gear, we are going for a little dive."

Chloe looked at her dad with her hands on her hips and a look of disappointment on her face: "Hey, what about me?"

"Oh sweetheart," Sam replied, "this could really be dangerous."

"Oh, you mean 'dangerous' . . . like this *whole mission?* Daddy, you know how many dives I have been on all throughout the Caribbean. Please, let me go."

Ms. Teal offered; "Sam you can take the lead. I will keep Chloe right beside me."

Sam looked deep into his daughters longing eyes and, after a brief moment, gave in: "Okay, however you have to stay close to Ms. Teal the entire way; there will be no wondering off."

Chloe clinched her fist and pulled her arm back: *"Yes."*

The Captain now addressed his first mate; "Seaman Coulson, bring us to the surface and maintain our position. James, stay vigilant for any unexpected visitors. Carlynn, search our computer banks for any details about sea life in this area; something here is very weird. Joseph, I would appreciate you and Tooney compiling a fully detailed topographical map of the ocean floor beginning with the canyon."

Nations Pride crested the surface and the top hatch opened. Chloe, of course, was the first one to reach the deck. Her father, Ms. Teal, Charlie, and Buddy followed. Sam double-checked their gear before motioning Corey to extend a special dive platform with wide steps that allowed easy entry into the water. One by one, they began submerging. That, of course, was when the unexpected started happening. Tooney raced to the hatch before Corey could close it, climbed out, and leaped into the sea. Carlynn panicked and, sprinting across the deck, attempted to dive in after her son. Joseph responded quickly and, catching her in mid air, pulled her back to the deck. Fortunately, Bondar was waiting just inside the entry to the cavern. When he saw the five divers, he started to turn to lead them when his incredible peripheral vision picked up Tooney splashing around. Bondar instinctively bolted to the surface and swept under the little boy. Tooney grinned from ear to ear, and having no fear of his circumstance, grabbed tightly on to Bondar's dorsal fin, pointed his index finger forward, and took a deep breath. The big shark submerged and began racing toward the spiraled opening, knowing he needed to get to the open-air expanse inside the cavern as quickly as possible. The dive team panicked as Tooney and Bondar passed them in the water with Jazzy and Baaya following close behind. Sam and his team kicked their fins as hard as they could to keep up. Joseph was struggling to calm Carlynn, wrapping her tight in his arms, gently rocking her back and forth: "Your son will be okay; we are the learners here. Your son somehow connects with this ocean and every creature in it. He has a gift that most parents would find annoying. You and your husband are very special people. Allowing young White Eagle to unlock his talents is what makes his spirit thrive. Consider yourself blessed that he is in *your* care. I am sure the shark will keep him safe."

Joseph's sage advice and loving concern proved the perfect recipe to settle Carlynn's anxiety. Joseph decided it would be best for them to work together on their assigned tasks.

Meanwhile, in the cavern, Sam literally tore his mask off when reaching the surface; *"Tooney,"* he shouted, *"Are you okay?"*

The little boy, who was already climbing on the cavern's ledges, turned and gave the Captain a thumb up. Sam quickly helped Buddy, Charlie, Joleen, and Chloe out of the water and onto a series of hewn steps, immediately texting a message from his wrist communicator to the ship that Tooney was safe. After removing their gear and having a chance to look around, in unison . . . they gasped. Half-man/half-fish images were lining one side of the enormous chamber's wall. This underwater mecca was definitely the vestige of an ancient kingdom.

Buddy's curiosity was the first to peak; "Hey Sam, is it just me or should there not be a source for the light down here? We swam down, and then up through a spiraled opening. By my calculations, this cavern should be pitch-black."

Sam and the rest of the team looked around. The light in the cavern was not bright; however, it was enough to make everything visible. The exact source of the luminescence was certainly a mystery. The team got in single file behind the Captain and started slowly circling the cavern's perimeter. Tooney jumped down from the image he was climbing on and followed. The second Sam rounded a particular corner, the dive knife he had strapped to the side of his leg violently ripped out of its sheath, flying across the cavern and sticking solidly to the outside rim of an unusually dark area of a wall completely devoid of structure. It was like looking at an empty black expanse of sky. Fortunately, for Sam and the rest, his knife was the only iron based metallic object any of them were carrying. Sam swallowed hard and responded, *"What the . . . ?"*

Joleen asked, "Is your leg okay?"

"Yeah," Sam responded, "I guess it is a good thing the sheath and buckle are made of plastic; I could have lost my leg. What can possibly be so magnetic that it can cause such a reaction?"

Tooney immediately replied, "Dark matter."

Charlie quickly took his sons hand and kneeled down in front of him; "Tooney, can you explain?"

Tooney looked over at Chloe whose eyes were, once again, begging for an explanation.

The little boy kept it simple: "Dark matter; it is locked in the asteroid. Light from the crystal opens the wavy window."

Buddy, Charlie, and Joleen quickly understood what Tooney was suggesting. Charlie explained it to Sam and Chloe: "Scientists have suggested that dark matter exists in the universe due to its enormous gravitational impact on planets and stars that cannot otherwise be explained. It is something that exists, but is obscure in space. A current scientific theory is that *light itself* is what triggers it. Light, oh how would you say . . . opens it, reveals its essence. There are so many unknowns that it is pretty much impossible to explain." Charlie took a moment to gather his thoughts.

Sam interrupted, "What asteroid, Tooney?"

"Sea floor of Bermuda triangle," Tooney replied.

The Captain's eyes narrowed; "Are you saying that dark matter is responsible for the Triangle?"

Tooney's head nodded in the affirmative.

All stood silent once again. Charlie however, quickly thought of a way to test what Tooney was describing, opening a Velcro pocket on his hip and taking out one of his new inventions. What looked like a flashlight was in effect, a mini replica of the laser he and Tooney had worked on to fire at the crystal. Transparent titanium made up the shell of the device, all other components consisting of equally non-magnetic materials. Its power source was comprised of a magnesium powder cap in a brass encasement, a special conical shaped diamond at the tip, and two scuppers designed into the front outer rim for energy release. The big question was; did it have enough power to affect the mysterious area on the wall? Charlie had everyone retreat around the corner of the cavern, urging each of them to cover their eyes while he put on some special eyewear, preparing to train the beam on a tiny corner of the dark mass. The light emitting from the tiny device lit up the cavern like a million halogen lamps. Instantly, about a six-inch spot of the dark expanse became liquid in appearance. The tiny laser's energy lasted only seconds and the intense, artificial light filling the cavern started funneling into the small, watery-appearing void as if sucked up by a vacuum cleaner. Charlie ran to the wall, quickly sticking his hand into the liquid structure, then withdrawing it almost as quickly. Tooney was right; Charlie's hand did not get wet. Charlie excitedly started yelling out, *"He's right!* My son has figured it out! He has exposed one of the most perplexing wonders of our universe! Sam we have to get the Raptor in the sky and *fire on that crystal!* There is no telling what it will unlock down here!"

Sam and the crew scrambled back around the cavern's ledge, captivated by the small area of shimmering mass. Pointing at the spot, Charlie busted out with an explanation; "You see; dark matter is best described, at least in my opinion, as a celestial adhesive, its power lying in what it has an attraction to . . . *light.* Its obscurity in space has made it impossible to test any proposed theory. One question that has scientists perplexed is; 'why can we not observe it?'" Charlie once again hesitated, his eyes still training on the quivering anomaly: "The reason must be . . . that there is no concentrated light from a significant enough energy source to reveal its presence. Just because something is not visible to the naked eye does nothing to prove it does not exist. After all, can any of us see radio waves or microwaves? We cannot see them but we know from their effect that they exist. So too with dark matter . . . its obscure effect on galaxies is undeniable. In addition, when you think about it, light in all its various forms is one of the principle products, or perhaps even building blocks, of the energy in our universe. From nuclear tests, we know how much energy, and its consequential light, even a single atom is harnessing. This little experiment at least proves how certain types of *concentrated* light can unlock things previously unknown. Our challenge now is whether we are brave enough to continue with our discovery. The only way to find out is to get the Raptor in the sky and fire on the crystal in the canyon. Who wants to volunteer to stay here and see what happens?"

Ms. Teal appreciated Charlie's enthusiasm, but was cautious; "Sam, how big would you say the area was that you saw engulfed in the fire that you described drew you and your ship to the location of the canyon?"

"Oh, I would have to say . . . about five miles. Why do you ask?"

"Well, you previously described the fire as circling the area, like a large ring."

"That is correct."

"I was just thinking; what if we were to get back to the ship and, starting from the canyon, set a circular vector based on say . . . a two and a half mile radius, to see if there are any more caverns like this one before we use the laser." Looking over at Charlie she asked, "Does that make sense?"

Charlie thought for a moment and agreed: "She's right Sam; think about the possibility that pockets of dark matter exist throughout this region? The gravitational forces resulting from the absorption of light from an enormous coronal mass ejection, literally a planet killer . . . could explain how a large asteroid managed to slip past the planet Jupiter and end up here. Really, the Triangle could be earth's impulse center, much like the electronic force that keeps our hearts beating."

Sam stood silent for a moment before replying. He looked over at Buddy Gold; "What is your opinion? These two make a valid point."

Buddy, deep in thought, took his time but finally acquiesced, "Hey, what do we have to lose?"

"Okay, then it's settled," stated Sam, "let's get back to the ship."

While the team was busy putting their dive gear back on, Bondar looked at Jazzy and asked, "What do you think they are doing now?"

Jazzy replied, "I have no idea, but I think you need to be ready for *you know who* to jump back into the water."

Sure enough, Tooney jumped off the ledge while the others were getting their masks and breathing apparatus' back on. Sam instinctively reached out to grab a hold of him but Bondar beat him to the punch. Tooney was already saddling up on Bondar's back and, with one hand grasping the shark's dorsal fin, was ready to ride. Pointing forward with the index finger of his free hand, Tooney had Bondar taking off at full speed. Chloe gazed into the water where Tooney jumped in, her eyes locking onto Jazzys. Chloe felt a strange connection with the young tiger shark and, even though she was suited up and could have climbed down the ledge, easing herself into the water, she leaped off the ledge, quickly clearing her mask. Jazzy smiled at Baaya and asked, "Do you think . . . ?"

Baaya replied, "Hey, why not try?"

Jazzy quickly swam beneath Chloe who grabbed onto her dorsal fin with both hands, and the two took off like a shot.

Sam yelled, "*Chloe . . . NO-O-O!*" He, Joleen, Buddy, and Charlie quickly lunged into the water, only the sharks who they figured would guide them back out of the cavern were already out of sight. Their only possible escort now was . . . Baaya. The little angelfish quickly made a pass around all of their masks and started leading the way.

Back on the surface Tooney quickly climbed on to the dive platform and started banging on the hatch. Joseph Hawk hurriedly opened it while Corey trained his cameras on the surrounding area. Suddenly, he gasped, seeing Chloe racing toward Nations Pride on the back of a tiger shark. She also grabbed onto the dive platform, pulling herself out of the water, and screaming out, *"What do you think of that, NEPTUNE?"*

Joseph and Carlynn hurried the kids down to the dive prep room to dry them off. Joseph then went back on top to await the arrival of the rest of the team. It took a while for the divers to show up because Baaya was in no hurry, knowing that the divers were dependent on her for direction. She swam slowly along, singing and swaying to her own little tune. Unfortunately, Sam and his team completely overlooked checking out the rest of the magnificent cavern, focusing only on following Baaya back to the boat. Had they taken some time to explore, they would no doubt have noticed its gold-lined ceiling and beautifully colored limestone columns. When the divers finally reached Nations Pride, Sam yanked off his mask, throwing it across the deck, and angrily blurting out, "Next time, I'm grabbing myself a *shark!* That angelfish is just too *stinking slow!*"

Buddy, Joleen, and Charlie burst out laughing while Corey Coulson kept his eyes trained on his screen, watching the three fish re-grouping with the humpback whale. He stared in disbelief, wondering; "What are the odds that those four are actually working together?"

Chapter 30

Captain O'Brien and his dive team took their time getting out of their gear. Sam informed Corey Coulson of Ms. Teal's idea of setting a circular, two and a half mile vector around the canyon. "It certainly makes sense Captain," Corey replied; "we know the co-ordinates from the canyon to here, so why not make this our starting point?"

"Good idea," answered the Captain. "Let's dive and get underway."

Before the craft fully submerged . . . BOOOM . . . an explosion rocked it hard.

"What in the world was that," shouted the Captain?

"I have no idea sir, but our hull monitors show no damage sir."

"Quick, pull up all images from our surface cameras!"

Just then, BOOOM . . . another explosion followed, its impact rolling Nations Pride over on her side.

Ms. Teal struggled to reach the helm, "What's happening Sam?"

"I will tell you as soon as our images come up on the big screen!"

Corey feverishly hurried to scan the surface while Sam took the helm. "There Captain, look there, that boat is racing right down our throat Sir! They must have picked up our dive team re-boarding the ship. Look at the guns on that thing! That is not your ordinary cruiser. What do you make of it Captain?"

Sam's face, blazing with anger, shouted out . . ."Pirates! Quick, Seaman Coulson, submerge and crank her to thirty-five knots! Level off at a depth of forty feet, and head straight for them!"

"But Captain . . ."

"*No buts,* Seaman Coulson, *Do as I say!* Charlie . . . quick, you and Tooney get to your controls, we are going to need the Raptor!"

Within fifteen seconds of submerging the Captain called out once again; "Seaman Coulson, use a sonar signal to calculate our distance to that boat!"

"But, Sir, we do not need to do that. We can use the cloaking scanner. Sending out a sonar signal will reveal our location."

"That is exactly what I am hoping for! Send the signal *now* Seaman Coulson!"

The ping rang out, loud and clear. Corey spoke under his breath, "So much for stealth technology."

"What is our distance," shouted the Captain?

Corey called out, "Two hundred yards and closing, Sir."

"Count to thirty and change course toward the canyon! Charlie, you and Tooney get the Raptor in the sky!"

With the click of a mouse, the engines on the Raptor roared to life, lifting it vertically from a specially prepared launching pad located on Ms. Teal's private island. At one hundred feet in altitude, the jet's thrusters kicked in, taking the aircraft to hypersonic speed in only fifteen seconds. Charlie called out, "The bird is in the air Captain!"

"Good, get her over the canyon and in firing position as quickly as you can. What is your estimate Tooney?"

Tooney replied, "Three minutes, fifteen seconds . . . Captain!"

Everyone's head on board Nations Pride cranked around when hearing Tooney's reply. Smiles suddenly graced all their faces, realizing that Tooney's social progress was well on track, giving Sam a sudden surge of confidence in his strategy.

"Seaman Coulson, as soon as we are within one mile of the canyon, verify our separation!"

The pirates' vessel unknowingly sped right over the top of Nations Pride, having nothing to detect her but the intermittent sonar pings. Within' one mile of the canyon, the sonar signal once again rang out, causing the rogue craft to immediately turn and follow.

"Captain; the enemy vessel is five hundred yards and closing Sir! That thing must be doing seventy knots!"

"Okay seaman Coulson, we have only one chance for this to work; as soon as we crest the top of the canyon, sound out one more signal and tuck us in tight inside the upper rim!"

He then turned to Tooney, "We are cutting this close, young man; when will the Raptor be in position?"

"Sixty-five seconds, Captain."

Once again, Sam smiled at Tooney. Charlie caught the captain's eye, and winked.

"Okay people, prepare for whatever comes," cautioned the Captain. "This is no drill . . . and I sure hope this plan works!"

When Nations Pride reached the canyon, Corey verified distance with one more ping and quickly maneuvered under a slight overhang just inside the rim. The pirate boat arrived only seconds later, traveling at an unbelievable speed, cresting the canyons rim and unknowingly heading straight for its center.

Tooney was then heard counting down . . ."five, four, three, two, and one . . . *fire!*"

The beam from the Raptor's laser streaked through the sky, hitting the crystal dead center, causing an intense explosion of blinding light shooting out in every direction. The Captain shouted, *"How long can we hold the beam Charlie?"*

"Not long, Sir!"

"Take 'er to the limit!"

Within seconds, the region began shaking violently, an enormous swirling vortex forming instantly directly over the center of the canyon. Intense light, surging through the surrounding caverns, set the ocean aglow with a miles wide ring of golden fire shooting a thousand feet into the sky. The pirate ship, being unable to escape the powerful current, began firing their guns wildly at the mysterious light coming from the laser into the canyon, thinking a military plane was targeting them. The pirate captain then ordered the firing of two stinger missiles. The dastardly weapons streaked into the sky; however, intense magnetism building up in the canyon coupled with the sudden formation of a waterspout caused an unexpected course reversal. Struggling in the grip of a massive watery funnel, the pirates panicked when both missiles turned in mid-flight, locking onto the heat coming off their boat's engines. The detonation blew the boat and its crew into oblivion.

The intense shock wave from the explosion slammed Nations Pride into the wall of the canyon.

"Damage report Seaman Coulson!"

"We're okay Captain; permission to get us out of here Sir!"

"Permission granted!" He then turned around; "Charlie, shut 'er down and get the Raptor back to home base!"

Corey fought to keep Nations Pride away from the vortex in the middle of the canyon. Still, her engines were no match for the current's intensity. The Captain called out, *"Joleen, any ideas?"*

Pointing to a specific spot on the instrument panel she responded, "Hit the *hyper-drive!*"

Sam quickly flipped open the clear plastic cover and yelled out, *"Hold on everyone!"* Slamming his hand down on a lighted mushroom-shaped switch, Nations Pride lunged forward from an enormous thrust of power, propelling them out of the grip of the surging water, and launching the craft skyward at least two hundred feet past the outer rim of the canyon. They splashed down just in time to catch a glimpse of the furious, miles wide ring of golden fire blazing in all its glory. However, within seconds of Charlie shutting down the laser, the flames from the mysterious inferno quickly retreated.

"Seaman Coulson, keep her *full ahead*," yelled the Captain!

"Aye, aye, Sir . . . Full ahead, Sir!"

The Captain spun around; "Did you say, Aye, Aye?"

"Sorry Sir, caught up in the moment Sir; you know, pirates and all."

Laughter exploded from the entire crew. Even Tooney was laughing so hard that he bounced out of his chair and onto the floor. Chloe's laughter caused her to begin choking. She addressed Corey and said, "That is why you will always be first mate, b-b-b-because, you . . . Seaman Coulson, know how to handle my dad."

Sam O'Brien sighed, realizing there was nothing he could say to calm his crew from their spontaneous reaction to Corey's wit. He looked around at the crew, leaned forward, and bracing himself against the counter surrounding the helm, started chuckling, realizing he had been upstaged by his first mate. He then looked at Joleen Teal, whose eyes were tearing up from her own reaction to the humor of the situation, and whispered to her with his hand shielding his mouth, "Go ahead, laugh it off . . . Huckleberry."

Joleen's eyes opened wide with a tinge of shock at his remark. She playfully smacked him on the arm for his flirtatious teasing.

"Okay, okay, let's get it together people. Seaman Coulson, set course back to the first cavern and resume our circular vector."

"But what about the canyon Sir; why don't we go back in and check it out?"

"Whatever happened in there, young man, will be evident by what else it affected in this region."

Corey obediently locked in the co-ordinates, making haste back to the cavern.

"I sure hope our friends are okay," remarked Chloe.

Joseph Hawk could read the concern of her heart. The friends she was referring to—were the fish.

Chapter 31

Big Jake urged, "Just a little further; come on, we can make it!" The violent percussion from exploding ordinance had Bondar and the girls dazed and disoriented. Jake was guiding them towards the cavern adjacent to the one where Kaihula hatched her young in order to provide shelter from the violent disturbance.

However, at the very moment they had reached the cavern, golden fire flashed out of the entry, engulfing them in its wake: *"AHHHHHH, HELP US!"* Jazzy and Baaya were panicking, screaming, lashing their bodies back and forth, and sensing they were perishing in the inferno. Bondar tried hard to calm the girls and help them ride out the experience, he having been through this once before. He shouted over their piercing cries, *"Hang on, you will be okay, you are not burning! It will all be over in a few moments!"*

Big Jake quickly swept Bondar and the girls beneath him with his long pectoral fins, locking them in tight to his underbelly.

When the mysterious flames finally subsided, Jazzy and Baaya were still shivering and crying their eyes out, holding on tight to Big Jake. He tried comforting them: "Everything is alright now, none of us are hurt. Quickly, follow Bondar into the cavern. You will be safe in there."

Bondar asked Jake; "Do you think you can make a run back to the area of the canyon and find out what happened to the boat?"

"Consider it done my friend. Though, you three had better take shelter deep in the cavern just in case this happens again."

"Good idea. We will do a little exploring until you return."

With that, Jake kicked into high gear, speeding back toward the canyon.

Entering the cavern's inner chamber, Bondar, Jazzy, and Baaya swam into an open expanse of blinding light, the walls of the cavern emitting an intense glow, causing them to shield their eyes. After adjusting to the unusually piercing illumination, colorful limestone columns lining the perimeter came into view. Jazzy, quickly scanning her surroundings, was the first to look up; "Well harness my tail and pull me ashore; will you look at that."

Bondar stopped suddenly and asked, "What did you say?"

"What is the matter, you never heard that one?"

Chuckling Bondar answered, "No . . . that is a new one on me."

"Well, don't let it prevent you from looking up."

When Bondar's eyes turned upward, he could not believe what he was seeing: a ceiling of shimmering gold. "I do not understand; I was in this cavern before and never noticed anything remotely like this."

Jazzy replied, "Yeah, but in the other cavern you claimed to have seen some sort of strange, glimmering window through which your friends disappeared, didn't you?"

Bondar's entire body stiffened. Slowly turning, he saw Jazzy and Baaya gazing into a shimmering expanse located behind some of the limestone columns. Its height spanned some twenty feet above and below the water line. Its width was about the same. "But, I only thought . . ."

"Thought what," asked Jazzy, "that the first cavern was the only one that contained a dimensional window? From your explanation of the symmetry of all the caverns, it would only make sense that they would have their similarities."

"You know, I think you must be related to Two Stars," replied Bondar; "You two think alike."

"Whatever. But I will tell you right now; I am not going to launch myself through like she did!"

Bondar frowned; "You don't have to, I will go in by myself. You two can stay here and wait for Jake."

"Oh sure, and leave us here to miss out on all the fun," ranted Baaya; "That is not happening! Look Jazzy, you may not want to go, but how do you know Socrates and the others are not just waiting for someone to come and help them? You *don't* know; and that is why we have to stay with Bondar!"

Baaya's outburst surprised Jazzy; however, the little angelfish was right. Bondar should not go alone. Jazzy thought for a moment. "Okay, how about this; I will go with Bondar and you stay here and wait for Big Jake. When the boat arrives, you try to get the little boys attention and lead him here."

"That is fair enough. Only, he had better not think he is going to have me pulling him along through the water! Angelfish don't do . . . rides!"

Bondar and Jazzy started laughing at Baaya's terse response. Bondar said, "Okay, little one, we understand. Just remember; our return is very uncertain and what you do from this point on could affect the ultimate outcome. Are you sure you are ready to take on that much responsibility?"

Baaya thought for a moment, her eyes drifting from one object to another; "Um, uh . . . Yep, I'm good. Enough talk now; you two get going!"

Bondar whispered to Jazzy, "She's a little dynamo, isn't she?"

"Oh-h-h-h . . . You have no idea."

Bondar and Jazzy wavered for but a moment, and then in the blink of an eye . . . disappeared.

Chapter 32

The hollow tumble through inner space put both sharks in a dreamlike trance, stripping their senses of all normal function. They simply had no equilibrium or perception of normal movement. The experience was very short lived though, as their freefall ended with a gentle plunge into the pristine waters of another majestic cavern. Both sharks floated lifelessly for a moment before regaining their mobility. Jazzy looked at Bondar, giggling over the experience: "Wow, I cannot wait to do that again."

"Let's just hope we get the chance. You do remember what I told you Kaihula said about this place, don't you?"

"Yes, but, look around. This place is too beautiful to be all that . . . terrifying."

"Never let first impressions deceive you. Now, follow me and stay vigilant."

Bondar took the lead through a labyrinth of beautiful mineral columns before entering the open expanse of a magnificent bay. It had been a long time since either of them had seen an actual shoreline. They swam into shallower water, bedazzled by the creatures lining the banks, when suddenly, Bondar recognized a familiar sound emanating through the water: *"They are here,"* he blurted out, *"they are here!"*

"Who is here," responded Jazzy?

"Quick, follow me!"

Bondar raced into the the center of the bay, desperately trying to follow the familiar clicking and chirping of dolphins. His eyes suddenly welled up in tears when he spotted none other than, Two Stars. Sensing an approach behind her, Two Stars spun around, yelling out, *"Bondar!"*

Enamored by the beautiful face he had missed so terribly, he gently grasped her fins, and kissing her, acknowledged: "I have never missed anyone so much in my life."

A spine-chilling surge of affection began racing through her, she hugging him tight and replying, "Ditto."

Socrates and Amaya arrived just in time to catch the two in an embrace of affection: "Oh, well," said Socrates, "I guess we should just . . . leave you two alone for a moment. We do understand."

Bondar chuckled, "I guess we're busted, huh?"

Socrates snickered, "Oh yeah, big time; how did you get here?"

"It is a crazy story; however, some humans showed up and somehow managed to energize the crystal. A terrible fight ensued with some other humans, and to make a long story short, we ended up in another cavern where a dimensional window opened. And you won't believe it; the little boy is back, you know, the one Schooner rescued."

Suddenly, Socrates' friends started appearing from all sides, Jibber picking up Two Stars' shout and relaying Bondar's arrival. Poker and Serine excitedly came streaking in together. Stopping abruptly, Poker said, "You sure took your time getting here. What, have you been sleeping in a cave or something?"

Bondar looked over at Socrates, rolled his eyes, and whispered, "He never changes, does he?"

"That would be a definite . . . no. By the way, who is your friend?"

Bondar turned and noticed Jazzy embarrassingly slumping into the background. "Jazzy, come on over here and let me introduce you. Everyone, this is Jazzy. She and her friend Baaya have been helping Big Jake and me to locate you. It is a good thing they showed up when they did, because it is doubtful we would have gotten this far without them. Enough talk, we need to get going; the window may not stay open all that long!"

Out of the background, a lone, tiny figure approached: "Bondar, is that you?"

Bondar's emotions paralyzed him for a moment. He spun around and clutched the little rockfish tight in his fins. Peetie was so overwhelmed that he could not even speak. Bondar asked, "So, how is my boy? Seeing you disappear through the window while helping Kaihula with her newborns made me feel so proud. When we get back, you can fill me in on what has been happening."

Socrates immediately interrupted, calling everyone forward: "Okay, this is our chance; let's all line up behind Bondar and get out of here!"

Amaya hesitated: "Socrates, do we have to leave? After all, we are finally safe and happy here. This place is certainly worth exploring . . . at least . . . for a little while."

Socrates could not believe Amaya's request: "Sweetheart, you have a Kingdom to manage. Do you not care what happens to all the fish that are relying on you for direction?"

Amaya slumped in sadness.

Bondar broke into the conversation; "Hey Socrates, conditions in Amaya's Kingdom are better than they have ever been. All the creatures are working in harmony with each other and, frankly, have come to grips with the fact that they will probably never see you again. What you, Amaya, Uncle Gnarls, and Poker set in motion is having an amazing effect on fish throughout the entire region. There are certainly those who miss you; however, it is not as though everything is on hold because you are not there." Then looking around he asked, "Hey, I thought Kaihula referred to this as a dimension of terror? From what I am seeing, this place is pretty . . . sweet."

Socrates responded, "It is a long story. I will fill you in on the details later." He then turned to Poker, and all the rest of his friends: "Are you feeling the same as Amaya?"

Anxious heads were bobbing up and down in the affirmative. That is when Jazzy panicked: "But what about my friend, Baaya? Bondar, we cannot just leave her! When Big Jake starts his migration, she will be all alone! There is no way she can survive all by herself! I am going back!" With that, she turned to hurry back to the cavern.

"Hold on!" shouted Bondar; "You are not going anywhere . . . *alone!"* Turning to Two Stars he shrugged; "I have to help her."

Two Stars smiled at the shark she loved and then addressed Jazzy: "I am going too; what we do, we do as a team." Turning to Amaya, she continued: "There is no need for the rest of you to take any more risks. We will work quickly to round up Jazzys' friend and get back as soon as possible."

Uncle Gnarls sighed, and in a broken voice stated; "Noni and I also want to return, to our home. We understand all of your desire to remain here . . . and that is okay. However, the memory of our son is too strong. We need to be there just in case, well, you know . . . you do understand, don't you?"

Socrates' heart sunk in sadness; "Yes Uncle, we understand." Then re-addressing the group he calmly stated, "Two Stars, Bondar, Jazzy, and I will take Uncle Gnarls and Auntie Noni back through. We will try to locate Jazzys' friend and get back before the window closes." Then looking at Kaihula and NuiMalu, he requested; "Please, take care of our friends."

Amaya broke down in tears. Kaihula gently reached out, and pulling Amaya close assured her, "Don't worry, little one, they will be just fine."

Suddenly Schooner sped forward; "I am going too and do not tell me no! I will risk anything to see that little boy again. Besides that, I will bet I can find Jazzys' friend faster than anyone."

Uncle Gnarls looked over at Socrates and said, "He does have a point. Schooner, Bondar, Two Stars, and Jazzy would make a good team."

Poker chimed in; "Well what about me? What am I, a floater in a bait ball?"

The chuckling started immediately. Socrates took his friend aside and explained; "Poker, our working together includes splitting up when necessary. Hang here with the plesiosaurs in case something happens to prevent us from getting back. You and Serine have to stay with Amaya. It is the only way I will ever have the strength for this."

Poker shrugged and said, "Alright; only, please, do not waste any time."

Socrates could read the extreme concern in Pokers' eyes. Leaving a best friend in an uncertain circumstance is always hard. Poker took a moment, sucking up his emotion; then winking at Socrates he suddenly blurted out, "Okay, let's do this thing! By the way, do you want to run that by me again?"

Everyone went into hysterics. Jazzy stared at the group in disbelief and said, "So, the stories are true. You two are the *Socrates* and *Poker* all of the stories are about."

Poker answered, "Well, it all depends on what you have heard. When you get back, you can share your take on the stories while we treat you and your friend to some delicious shrimp. How does that sound?"

"Really, that would be wonderful. I cannot wait."

Socrates frowned while Serine, Two Stars, and Zippee shot daggers out of their eyes at Poker. Nevertheless, neither of them could resist the temptation to see the trick played on newcomers.

Bondar, Two Stars, Jazzy, and Schooner then started toward the cavern while Socrates took a moment, kissing Amaya goodbye. With that, he, Uncle Gnarls, and Auntie Noni hurried to follow their young companions.

Chapter 33

The brief tumble back through inner space felt enthralling to Socrates. It was like the ultimate dream sensation, a brief shutdown of all consciousness. The touchdown though, came all too soon. Within seconds, he and his friends were back, Uncle Gnarls recognizing the old cavern. He used to sneak away and play there when he was young.

Socrates abruptly asked Jazzy; "Is this where you left your friend?"

"Yes. Follow me and I will show you where Big Jake was supposed to lead the boat."

The cavern was still emitting its strange glow from the effect of the laser on the crystal. Once outside the caverns entry Jazzy called out, *"BAAYA, where are you?"*

A tiny voice came out of a crevice in the face of a rock formation: "Well that didn't take long. Are you sure you went anywhere?"

Socrates smiled and whispered to Bondar, "Do I sense a little attitude here?"

Bondar responded, "You think?"

Jazzy continued, "Where is Big Jake? Did he find the boat?"

Baaya responded, "Oh, you mean the one you cannot see even if you are looking right at it? Well, hmm, Jake certainly has not arrived and I have not been run over by an invisible craft the whole, what, ten minutes you have been gone!"

Jazzy looked hard at Baaya and asked, "Okay, what is your problem?"

Baaya started crying and answered, "The problem is, I am scared to death! There are some strange looking creatures hanging out around here and I thought one of them was going to eat me! That is my problem!"

Just then, Uncle Gnarls and Noni swam into view and Baaya started screaming: "AWWW . . . See . . . *That* is who I have been hiding from!"

"What are you talking about? This is Uncle Gnarls and Auntie Noni. They are with us."

"Yeah, well, they sure have some *scary looking* relatives!"

At that moment, from behind the group, a soft, penitent voice called out, "Mom, Pops, is . . . that . . . you?"

Gnarls and Noni froze from the pure shock of hearing a familiar voice from the distant past. Their eyes started welling up in tears, hesitating for a moment to turn around because of the extreme pain of a flood of negative memories. Gnarls pulled Noni to his side, holding her tight, slowly turning his head toward the voice. For the first time in his long life, he did not know how to respond.

The trembling voice continued; "Mom, dad, I am so sorry. Please forgive me. I was so young and did not know what I was doing. I had no idea what Monegore was up to. However, it is no excuse. I was so arrogant. I could not see how important your wisdom of years meant to the reef's balance. Please, please, forgive me. My life is so empty without you."

With that, Bohunk broke down crying. "Oh mom, dad, please forgive me; I cannot take this . . . isolation."

Gnarls and Noni responded to the plea in a heartbeat. They both wrapped themselves around their son, responding purely from parental instinct: "There, there," said Noni in a sweet, comforting voice, "your father and I are right here. We will all be okay. Believe me son, we never forgot you."

Socrates looked on with wonderment, absorbing the significance of this moment. Uncle Gnarls and Auntie Noni were the epitome of love and forgiveness.

Gnarls turned to Socrates; "I am rethinking our position on returning home."

He then looked at his mate, her eyes filling with joyful tears, "Sweetheart, let's take him out of here; we can make a fresh start. We need a . . . new beginning."

At that moment, four more figures slowly appeared out of another crevice in the rock. Bohunk meekly introduced his family; "Mom, dad, this is my mate and our three young ones."

Noni's face shone with a brightness that rivaled the light from the laser. She turned to Gnarls and said, "We have to get them out, now!"

Gnarls quickly turned to Socrates, "Please, you know we want to help, but we may not have another opportunity."

"Go Uncle, we've got this. We will be right behind you. Hurry now!"

While Gnarls rushed his family back into the cavern and toward the window, Big Jake came into view with Nations Pride following him on the surface. Schooner flipped when he saw Tooney's head poking out above the hatch. Hurrying over, he accidentally rammed his snout into the side of the nearly invisible craft. "What the . . . ! What did I hit?"

Baaya started laughing; "Oh, yeah, it feels so good to have a little company, doesn't it?"

Schooner said, "I sure am glad you can find some humor in this, you little twerp."

Aboard Nations Pride, Tooney climbed out of the hatch, instantly spotting Schooner. Sam O'Brien was right behind him and reached out a fraction of a second too late to prevent Tooney from leaping into the water. In a split second, Tooney emerged, flying out of the water on the back of his amazing little friend. Schooner and Tooney picked up where they left off, the young dolphin porpoising in and out of the water, Tooney holding on to his dorsal fin with one hand while waving the other high in the air. The crew quickly climbed out of the hatch to catch the excitement. Carlynn and Charlie could not believe what they were seeing. What were the odds of Tooney finding the same young dolphin in this seemingly endless expanse of open ocean? A liberating realization swept over them; nothing on this earth is beyond Tooney's reach. While they watched, Corey Coulson called the Captain back to the helm. "Captain, come quick, you gotta' see this!"

Sam scurried back down the hatch and over to the helm.

Corey continued, "Isn't that the same hammerhead, tiger shark, and angelfish we saw earlier?"

"It certainly looks like them. It appears as though they have brought along some additional company." He then called out; "Joleen, hurry down and check this out!"

Chloe followed Joleen back down the hatch and directly over to the video monitor, marveling at the piscine attention to Schooner and Tooney racing across the water.

Buddy Gold suddenly got a strange look on his face, scampering back down the hatch, and logging on to his laptop. "That's it," he shouted, "that's it! The markings on the ship's bell that Chloe bought are not Spanish. They are," he stopped for a moment, checking out a linguistics program: "they are . . . just a moment . . . yes, yes, that is it; the markings are an archaic form of *Portuguese*. Sam, look at this. Here are some of the word groupings. Now look at the bell. The character arrangement is a perfect match, from right to left, much like Hebrew. Get me a digital camera, I have an idea."

Sam called out, "Chloe, did you bring your camera with you?"

"I have it in my bag."

"Quickly sweetheart, hand it to Buddy."

Buddy took the camera from Chloe and, placing the bell in the center of the table, snapped five photos of the markings from various positions around the table starting from right to left. He then took out the SD card, plugging it into his computer, and arranging the character photographs into one complete sentence. He then proceeded to scan it into the ship's mainframe. It took only a moment for the interpretation to come across the screen: "In search of Golden Atlantis, the City of Dancing Fire."

Buddys' face turned stark white, his body trembling. All eyes were staring at the video monitor in disbelief when Buddy shouted at the top of his voice, *"Yes, oh yes . . . we found it! It is right here! We are in the middle of the lost city of—Atlantis!"*

Sam called out to Corey, "Anchor in right here Seaman Coulson. Put all monitors on maximum detection. We need to make sure we do not have another incident like we did with the pirates."

Corey did not move, his headset on, his face showing concern. Sam looked at him; "Did you hear what I said Seaman? Get busy and set the anchor!"

"Sir, you need to hear this."

Corey clicked his computer on high-def audio, raising the decibel level. Sam listened closely: "What is that? Where is it coming from? Charlie," he shouted, "quick, get down here and listen to this!"

Charlie immediately climbed down the hatch, Corey handing him a pair of earphones in order to drown out all other noise. He listened intently for a moment then asked; "Corey, where is the signal coming from?"

Corey scanned his monitor for the audio source and with a slight glitch in his voice replied, "From the uh . . . cavern, sir."

Sam asked, "What kind of signal is it Charlie? Do you recognize it?"

Charlie shrugged with no immediate answer . . . though Buddy had a hunch. He took the earphones from Charlie. After several moments of honing in on the faint transmission, closing his eyes tightly to concentrate, a look of concern swept over his face, he suddenly responding, "Remember what I related about the National Geophysical Data Center picking up an early form of radio signal decades ago? Well, I think we have found the signal's source. Quick, Corey, give me something to write on."

Corey handed Buddy some sticky notes and a pen. Buddy then shuffled it off to Charlie: "Here, take this, I have an idea."

Buddy's ears were straining while listening to the methodical message. A distinct pattern of dots and dashes were now becoming obvious: Buddy looked over at Sam, "It's Morse code!" Then turning to Charlie he said, "Write this down!"

Charlie fumbled with the pen for a moment but then focused only on Buddy.

Buddy started deciphering the message:

"Mayday . . . Mayday . . . Mayday . . . Survivors . . . Anders Highley . . . Aviator . . . July 18, 1945. Mayday . . . Mayday . . . Mayday . . . Survivors . . . Anders Highley . . . Aviator . . . July 18, 1945." The same message continued, repeatedly.

After dictating the same message at least a dozen times, Buddy took the headset off, stared at the floor for a moment, then slowly raising his head and looking over at Sam, proposed; "Captain, I'm afraid our discovery expedition . . . has just turned into a rescue mission."

The Captain took a seat, reflecting on his crew's next move. After a brief and quiet contemplation, he clasped his hands, stood back up and gave the order; "Okay people, let's suit back up; we are going in. Oh, and Charlie, try to coax your son back to the side; we at least have to get a wet suit on him. Corey, keep recording the message and let us know of any changes." Then re-addressing Charlie he added; "You are going to have to stay on board as team leader. You, Joseph, James, and Carlynn are going to have to keep a sharp eye out. If you have to, move the ship away from this location and get the Raptor in the sky. Scare the daylights out of anyone approaching this area. We need to buy some time in order to see what we are up against in the cavern. We are going to need at least an hour to check this out."

There was no hesitation from the crew. Charlie and Carlynn quickly coaxed their son back to the ship. As nervous as they were to allow Tooney to accompany the dive team into the cavern, both parents knew the importance of feeding Tooney's inner spirit. To shut him down, now, could send him into an emotional tailspin. After getting Tooney zipped up in his wet suit, Charlie held his finger out to his side. Tooney's eyes focused on it while Charlie brought his finger back in front of his own face, establishing eye contact: "Tooney, we are counting on you to help the Captain. Make us proud, son."

In that special moment of connection with his father, Tooney threw his arms around Charlie, hugging him tight. He then proceeded to do the same with his mother. However, this time he cupped his mothers face in his hands and kissed her. Carlynn's face was glowing while Tooney said, "Chloe taught me that. I watched her one day with her dad." Tooney then scanned the area surrounding the ship, located Schooner, and leaped into the water. Schooner hurried over, and in an instant, began speeding around the craft with Tooney on his back.

Sam and his team of divers emerged from the hatch with all their gear in tow. Charlie and Carlynn helped the divers check their equipment before seeing them off. Once the team was ready, Sam implored James; "There is a lot riding on what we find. Do not hesitate to use all means necessary to avoid a confrontation. It is possible that an orbiting satellite could have picked up our fight with the pirate ship. Right now, secrecy is our greatest asset. He then shook hands with James, Joseph, and Charlie. Approaching Carlynn he said, "What an amazing young man you have raised. Believe me when I say, I will protect him with my life." He then gave Carlynn a big hug, turned, and joined his team getting into the water. Not one moment had passed when Corey called out, "Hey guys get down here, pronto!"

James, Joseph, Carlynn, and Charlie hurried back down the hatch and over to the big screen monitor. Awaiting the Captain's dive team was none other than the same group of fish Corey had been monitoring since their arrival. "Watch this people, and then tell me something strange is not going on."

When Sam, Joleen, Chloe, and Buddy entered the water, Tooney and Schooner shot past them and submerged into the canyon. On the starboard side of the ship, Socrates,

Bondar, Two Stars, Jazzy, and Baaya briefly met up with Big Jake: Socrates spoke first; "Thank you Jake for what you have done. We are not sure whether we will ever be back. There is so much to learn and a lot more mystery to unravel. Hopefully, someday, we will meet up again."

Bondar struggled with what he was going to say. He finally swam up to Jake and whispered, "you big knot head—stay safe, huh."

Jake came back, "Yeah, uh, you too; and, try and keep an eye out."

"Oh, that's a good one. You probably took at least a day to come up with that."

"Yep, I have been working on it ever since I went to find the boat. By the time you get back I will probably have some new material."

"I can hardly wait."

Baaya now swam up to Big Jake and asked, "Please, can we do our trick just one more time?"

"Okay little one, you know the drill. Get moving."

Baaya sped back to Big Jakes fluke, poking her head through the hole. Jake pushed down extra hard, shooting Baaya into the sky screaming and laughing; she then tucked and landed in a perfect dive. Kissing Big Jake on his face she lamented; "I am going to miss you so much, but someday, I don't know how, we will return and I am going to come looking for you. I love you Big Jake."

"I love you too, squirt."

With that, Socrates and his friends turned to catch up to the divers, and surrounding them in a tight formation, disappeared into the cavern.

"Did you see that," said Corey excitedly? "Did I not tell you something strange was going on with the fish? They have been coordinating all of this!"

Joseph Hawk candidly addressed the young mariner: "You are catching on; never suppose other creatures are completely unintelligible. Keep observing . . . and you will keep learning."

Meanwhile, Sam, Joleen, Chloe, and Buddy entered the incredible expanse of the cavern's interior. The presence of unexplainable incandescent light, beautiful limestone columns, and a ceiling of pure gold, caught the dive team by surprise. The stories of the lost city of Atlantis, although intriguing, could never prepare one for a display of magnificence such as this. Sam stifled his gawking and started looking around for Tooney. That is when he noticed Socrates and the other fish staring into the empty void of the dimensional window. Sam quickly motioned for the rest of the team to move toward the anomaly when he started to panic, frantically scouring the area for the possibility of an open-air expanse with breathable air. Tooney had entered the cavern without any breathing apparatus. Sam suddenly cringed, realizing that Tooney and the dolphin had only one way out. Sam stared into the quivering mass fronting him and the dive team, thinking only of his promise to Carlynn . . ."I will guard him with my life." Using the communicator on his wrist, he looked over at Joleen and typed out; "Keep Chloe safe. I have to go in after Tooney. Tell Carlynn I *will* keep my promise."

The message transmitted not only to Joleen but also to the communicators on the wrists of Chloe and Buddy. Buddy sternly replied, "Not without me, Captain!"

Sam pulled his daughter over to him, took off his mouthpiece, and kissed her on the head. He then took Chloe's hand and, placing it in Joleen's, gave the two a determined smile, turned, and swam straight into the void. Buddy gave Joleen a nod and followed. Chloe panicked, and yanking her hand away from Joleen, bolted after her father and disappeared. Socrates, reading Joleen's alarmed and helpless response, swam quickly in front of her, his piercing eyes locking onto her's, forcing her to back away. Yielding to the extreme emotion of the moment, Joleen sensed a strange connection with the large cod, temporarily calming her. She gently tapped her chest with her fist, and then, pointing her finger at Socrates, muttered a quiet plea under her breath; "You . . . please, bring them home."

Socrates slowly backed away, motioning to his friends with a slight twitch of his head, and vanished.

Joleen floated motionless for several minutes, her mask filling with tears, thinking only of how she would explain her team's disappearance to Tooney's parents. A sickening fear and numbness swept over her while watching the bright, shimmering corridor suddenly turn opaque and harden into stone. For a brief moment, she felt paralyzed. Yet her strong, aggressive nature began surging, and she made haste back to the ship.

Upon seeing Carlynn and Charlie waiting on the dive platform, she began stressing over breaking the news about the others, especially Tooney.

"Hurry;" shouted Carlynn, "we don't have much time!"

Joleen was puzzled; Carlynn did not even ask about her son. Charlie explained while helping with her gear: "Only moments ago, we received a message from Sam. The four of them are safe. Let's get below; we have to leave the area, *now!*"

With what was left of the crew safely onboard, James secured the hatch and, in an instant, Corey had Nations Pride submerged and speeding away.

Coming up next:

Battle for Atlantis

GLOSSARY OF HAWAIIAN NAMES USED FOR CHARACTERS AND THEIR MEANING

Kai'Hula	Tide Dancer
Nui'Malu	Big Protector
Ka'e'a'e'a'	Hero, Champion
Kai'mana	Power of the Ocean
Keapualani	Heavenly White Flower
Mau	Persevere
Makana	Gift
Manawa-heihei (little Manny)	Time Racer